The Last Boss' Daughter

SAM MARIANO

This is a work of fiction. Names, characters, businesses, places, events and incidents are either the products of the author's imagination, or used fictitiously. Any resemblance to actual persons, living or dead, or actual events is purely coincidental.

The Last Boss' Daughter Copyright © 2017 by Sam Mariano

All rights reserved.

ISBN-13: 978-1546962083

No part of this book may be reproduced in any form or by any electronic or mechanical means, including information storage and retrieval systems, without written permission from the author, except for the use of brief quotations in a book review.

DEDICATION

To my brother, David.

May the words keep flowing, even when life gets stressful. ;)

Check out Sam Mariano's other titles

MAFIA ROMANCE
Accidental Witness (Morelli Family, #1)
Surviving Mateo (Morelli Family, #2)
Once Burned (Morelli Family, #3)
Family Ties (Morelli Family, #4)

NEW ADULT
Because of You (#1)
After You (#2) (coming 2017)

TABOO ROMANCE
Irreparable Damage (#1)
Irreparable Lives (#2)
Irreparable Box Set

STANDALONE CONTEMPORARY ROMANCE
Beautiful Mistakes

CHAPTER ONE
Annabelle

There's an old junkyard in Brooklyn that doesn't mean much to anyone but me.

My father used to bring me when I was young. Behind the old, beaten fence stands a huge oak tree with an apple tree just behind it. Dad hung up a rope swing just for me and before long it became my favorite place in the world. Dad would grab two apples, toss me one, and push me on the swing while I told him about my day or my dreams or my dolls or the boy I liked — whatever I wanted to talk about. My dad was a busy man, so having his undivided interest in those moments… well, it was special to me.

Every year on the anniversary of his death, I come back. I trespass on the land that's no longer ours, steal two apples from the tree, and swing on the swing that the new owners never took down. While I'm there, eating stolen apples and swinging on someone else's swing, I talk to my dad. Of course he isn't *there*, but I talk to him anyway.

Only this year, something is different.

The junkyard isn't abandoned.

I'm unsure what to do at first. Lights are on inside and a few vehicles are parked in front of the building. The alarming part is the two armed guards stationed by the rickety old fence, guarding the entrance. All this for a yard full of rust? There can't be much left of the cars at this point.

The guards go on alert as I walk by. I pick up the pace, my heart pounding as one takes a threatening step forward. What the hell? I'm not sure what to do now. I could go home and forget my annual tradition, but…

I reach the end of the road before I decide, fuck it. Those guys saw me keep walking, so they're probably back to relaxing and bullshitting with each other. I don't want inside the fence anyway; I want to go behind it.

I have to go about it a different way, that's all. Usually I walk right in, cut through the hole in the fence at the back, but my instincts tell me before I even get there, that hole is probably gone. Whatever's inside, someone wants their privacy.

Cool with me.

I couldn't care less.

My curiosity isn't even piqued.

I just want a few minutes on my swing. I just want to steal two apples, then I'll be on my way.

It may be dangerous. Little red warning flags, but fuck those, too. I'm going on my swing. I haven't let dangerous men stop me from doing what I want in 26 years, so why start today?

And I make it. I cut through an alley, go behind a building, hustle across a clearing, and I'm along the side of the fence, safely out of the view of the guards. Smiling faintly to myself, filled with an unfamiliar sense of peace and victory, I pluck a pair of apples from the tree, climb up on the seat of my swing and push off. I'm a little less sure about talking to my dad with the security on the place, but as long as I'm quiet it should be okay.

"Hey, Dad," I murmur, hooking my left arm around the rope. "It's been a while."

For a moment, I stop, words clogging my throat. As much as I love the idea of telling Dad about my life, I realize things have gotten so bad that I don't *want* to tell him.

Instead, I say, "Do you remember when I was 14 and I finally figured out the whole Mafia thing? How I was so conflicted about it, and… and I felt like my image of you was sort of damaged, and it was so morally reprehensible to do the things I realized you were responsible for?"

I remember an argument we had during that time, in the car on the way home from the junkyard. My arms crossed in anger, telling him, "I would never do those kinds of things, not for any amount of money."

My dad shook his head, seeming vaguely irritated with my naiveté, and told me, "You think that now, but everyone has a price."

"I don't," I assured him, vehemently.

He nodded, not agreeing. "We'll see."

He never did get to see, since he was killed two years later. I hadn't sold out by then. Not what you would expect of a daughter of a criminal organization, but I was actually a goody goody. Hadn't even had my first kiss until after he died.

As it turned out, life's sharper corners poked holes in most of my ideals, like my father predicted they would.

Clearing my throat, I say, "Remember when you told me, even though our family was our kind of family, that if I really didn't like it, and it really made me unhappy, I didn't have to have any part of it? I could have a normal life with my little ideals and live blissfully unaware of the goings on?" He couldn't answer, of course, but I nod anyway. "I think if you would've lived, that might've been true."

I don't get to further speculate, share, or reminisce. The sound of dying leaves crunching beneath heavy boots serves as adequate warning. I launch off the swing and turn with my back to the tree so I can look my attacker in the face, a particular habit of mine.

I like to unsettle them, if I can.

This guy doesn't seem unsettled. A blonde, short-haired guard stands, legs braced, large gun trained on me, ready to attack.

"Over here!" the guy calls over his shoulder.

Another guard comes around the side of the building, leaves crunching beneath his heavy, black boots. He's bigger than this guy—a lot bigger. Looks like he's all broad shoulders and lean muscle underneath all that gear.

He doesn't stop next to his friend, but keeps coming. I lurch back when I realize he's coming *at* me, but there's no time—and no point trying—to get away with him right on me. If I run, he'll give chase. And probably tackle me. Bruises. Soreness. Nah, not worth it.

I can just explain myself. I don't want the nuke codes or dead bodies they have inside, I only wanted a few minutes on the swing from my childhood.

"This has all been a misunderstanding," I attempt.

Blondie is inexplicably out for my blood and enthuses, "That's the same girl that just walked by!"

Someone get the man a detective license.

The wall of man stalking toward me is similarly unimpressed with his partner's deductive skills, but there's no time to consider that—or even the unexpected handsomeness in front of my face, the chiseled features, the short pony tail of golden hair, or his overall largeness. I wasn't initially intimidated by his strength, but the closer he gets, the more worrisome a detail it seems.

"Who are you?" he demands, pressing one large hand against my chest, effectively pinning me down.

My wide eyes focus on his hand as he holds me against the tree and starts patting me down.

"I—I'm not carrying," I manage through my surprise. "I don't even own a weapon."

"Who are you?" he repeats.

"Annabelle?" I offer.

He gives me a dead look, but that may just be his face. He turns me around, belly to tree, and pats me down that way, too.

Then I'm spun back around, but before I can imagine he's satisfied that I'm not dangerous, he comes forward, using his whole body to smash mine against the tree.

"Whoa," I mutter, unprepared for the impact.

"Get Raj," he calls back to Blondie. I can't see him through the wall of chest impeding my view, but I hear Blondie break into a run.

I swallow, my heart in my throat, but a smile creeps across my lips.

I don't react to things properly. It's been a struggle for a little less than half my life. It started at my dad's funeral when I was beyond devastated, but I didn't want to cry so I told jokes. People thought I was having a nervous breakdown. I've adapted "fake it till you make it" as a coping mechanism. It pisses Paul off to no end.

As if egged on, the guard bucks against me, smashing me even harder against the tree.

Not the intended reaction, I sense a poorly timed stirring in my loins.

I decide to use it. "Watch out there, buddy. If you're looking to turn me on, you're on the right track."

For the briefest fraction of a second, a glimmer of surprise crosses his face before the mask of stoicism slips back into place.

He leans back a step and lifts my 130 pounds with the ease I lift a fork. Nudges my legs apart and pushes between them aggressively, like he's going to push right through my clothes and fuck me there against the tree.

"Still turned on?" he grinds out.

Still stoic. Can't tell what he's going for here. Trying to scare me? Maybe he's trying to call my bluff. I wasn't bluffing, but there's no reason for him to suspect that.

In response, I smile and wrap my legs around his waist, using my heels to pull him even tighter against me. It's exhilarating, courting actual danger like this. I'm truly getting turned on, which is *so* inappropriate, and I wish I could find even a single fuck to give.

The guard scowls, but interest lingers there. "What are you playing at?"

"Not even playing." My eyes move over the muscular curves of him, the handsome face, the good hair. "I mean, look at you. You're hot. I'm not trying to soften you up or anything, just stating the facts." I crane my neck to peek over his shoulder before giving him a little wink. "How long do you think we have until your buddy gets back?"

Less intense, less guarded, he asks again, but this time less as if he's interrogating me and more like he actually wants to know, "Who are you?"

"Annabelle Covello," I tell him, even though I'm still not sure it's a great idea.

He recognizes the name and his scowl comes back, his interest draining. "Covello?"

I nod, resigned.

Footsteps again, more than one set. Blondie says, "Here she is."

His new companion says, "Jesus, Liam, get off the poor girl."

Liam, I surmise, is the guard between my legs, because suddenly my feet hit solid ground again and he backs away, as commanded.

"I apologize, miss," the man says, offering an apologetic smile. "We've had some security concerns lately, and I fear these two may have been a little overzealous. I hope—"

I cut him off because I can't believe who I'm looking at. "Raj?"

He frowns, eyeing me speculatively.

Raj Ahuja, the man who'd run the junkyard with my dad all those years ago. The years must not have been kind to him; it looks like he's aged 20 years in the 10 since I've seen him.

"I'm sorry, have we met?" he asks.

"I'm Annabelle C—Annabelle De Luca." Of course that wasn't the name I'd just given the guard, so he scowls in my direction. "My dad was John De Luca."

He knows who I am now and it seems like he expected me to still be 16. "Annabelle?"

I nod. "I didn't know you still owned this place. I thought after Dad…"

"I bought them out. It didn't take a lot, the shop wasn't much."

I agree, but I look to the guards. "That's what I always thought until I saw SEAL Team Six over here guarding the entrance."

Raj gets uncomfortable. "Yes, I…"

Since he doesn't seem eager to finish that sentence, I do it for him. "Security concerns, I heard."

His gaze moves away from me to the swing, still swaying ever so slightly. "Your dad used to bring you out here when you were younger, didn't he?"

I nod, but I'm not sure how much to say. I would've expected Raj to be happy to see me—I had loved him when I was a kid, and even into my teens we had remained friendly, always joking around when I came to the shop, which was admittedly less with every year that passed. He has a son a little younger than me, sometimes he'd bring him and we'd play baseball in the open grass by my tree swing.

This Raj still seems tense though, on his guard, not the same Raj I joked around with back then.

"Well, I should probably go," I say. "I'm sorry to have caused a whole… incident," I add, gesturing around to the armed giants.

"Yes, I'm sorry about that." He pauses, as if unsure whether or not to go on. "But, Annabelle? It's not a good idea for you to come back here."

I frown, taken off guard. Ordinarily I'm good at dodging undesirable feelings, but this is so unexpected that I am slightly offended. "Oh."

"Nothing personal."

"It seems personal. I only come…" I want to continue, but stop short. No. This isn't the Raj I knew, I'm not going to share anything vulnerable with him.

He ages another year or so before my eyes. Sighing, he looks at me like he has to put down his favorite dog. "Go home,

Annabelle. And don't come back."

CHAPTER TWO
Liam

"Follow her." I watch Raj as he sinks heavily into his seat behind the desk. "Make sure she isn't reporting back to her stepfather."

I know which way she went and I don't want to get too close, so I know I have a minute. "All right."

"Don't hurt her," he specifies, shooting me a look. I can tell he didn't appreciate the scene he came upon outside. I wouldn't even begin to know how to explain it to him, so I don't try.

Then, shoving a stack of papers irritably across the desk, he says, "Not yet, anyway."

"How long do you want me to stay on her?"

"The rest of the night. Just in case she anticipates this and does something else to throw you off."

I hesitate. "I really don't think she was up to anything. When we got out back, she was just swinging and eating an apple."

I could still smell the apple on her breath when I got so close to her and she inexplicably tried to… do whatever the hell she'd been trying to do.

"Well, let's hope. But we need to be sure."

I nod and leave to trade my large weapon in for something

more discreet, then I shed my top layer of gear. I can't wait too long and lose her, either. Even assuming I found her, I wouldn't know the trail she took—any stops, phone calls, hurried texts.

There's nothing to worry about though, as I find her quickly. I send a text to Lance to follow me with a car. A quick check shows she lives in Jersey and that means we're not going to be walking the whole way. I tell him to throw the audio equipment in the back seat, just in case.

As far as I can follow her—down into the subway, but not *on* the subway, since I'll be spotted—she doesn't do anything alarming. No phone calls, no texts. She doesn't even fiddle with apps to distract herself.

She looks sad. There's a sort of sag to her shoulders, her mouth set in a practiced frown. There's nothing about her that gives me any inkling she might be spying for her stepfather or anyone else.

Raj said her dad died, and that he used to bring her to the swing when she was little. Maybe that's why she was there, for sentimental purposes.

Her two last names confuse me. There was no time to ask Raj about it.

As she waits for the subway doors to open, I try to figure out how to play this. Given the stops, she could be heading into the city to shop, or she could be heading home. For half a second, I consider blowing my stealth all to hell and just approaching her. I could probably get the information I wanted by watching her closely while I simply asked, and if not, there was always brute force. Of course, on a subway full of people that wouldn't be as effective, and it wasn't likely she would follow me into some secluded alley to chat.

I wasn't able to peg her, given the briefness of our encounter and her odd reaction to it, so I don't take that chance.

Once she's in the subway car, I call Lance and give him the subway stops.

"Put someone on the train in case she surfaces. I'm gonna take the car."

I head for Jersey, because I think she's going home.

She doesn't surface at the stops, and before long it's clear I was right. Someone did get on the subway with her at the next stop, someone she wouldn't have recognized as watching her, and they verified that she hadn't done anything suspicious. Checked her phone once, they reported, but seemed to only be checking the time.

I wanted to get to her home first anyway because it could be a fortress. I didn't know if she lived with her mom and stepdad or had her own place. If it was the former, evading notice would take a little doing.

But when I get to the address, there's no fortress. It isn't some big, cushy, well-protected mansion, but a little blue house with too many windows. Wasn't going to be hard to keep an eye on her.

A green truck sits in the driveway and the back right of the house is well lit. I double check with the person tailing her that she's heading my way, then I park up the street and wait.

My mind wanders back to the tree, pushing between her legs. I had to believe she was playing me, but there was a certain gleam in her brown eyes that made me consider maybe she wasn't.

I couldn't let her know I was there, of course, but I wouldn't mind if I could. Show up on her doorstep, have the little act she pulled earlier be real. Follow her inside, push her up against her living room wall…

I shift in my seat, attempting to accommodate my budding erection. No point thinking about all that. I need to observe and not interrupt her routine so I can see if she reaches out to her stepfather.

Ugh, her stepfather. Fucking Pietro Basso. Just thinking his name swiftly kills my arousal. Fucker's a rabid dog that needs to be put down.

Before long, Annabelle pulls into her driveway in a beat-up little blue car—not what I expected her to drive with the kind of money her family has.

I watch her climb out and size up her wardrobe, now that I'm thinking about it. She looks cute in her casual jeans and gray sweater, but nothing about her outfit seems especially good quality.

Does she not have money? How would she not have money?

Since she's heading inside, I turn on the amplifier and there's a sudden—if crackling—burst of noise, as if I had walked right into the house with her.

There's a sound like keys being dropped, then something unclear in the background.

"Yeah," Annabelle says, her voice lifeless.

"Where were you?" I make out. The voice moves closer, so I can hear better toward the end of the question than the beginning.

"Had stuff to do. What are you doing home so early?"

"What's that supposed to mean?" the other voice asks. A male.

"I thought you were going to be out until later."

"No. I said I'm *going* out later."

"Oh." She doesn't seem interested and there's silence for a few minutes. I wait for her to make a phone call or mention something about what she'd just experienced at the junkyard, but it never happens.

A few minutes later, the male voice comes back, asking her if she cleaned the bathroom, "because it looks like shit."

I don't know who he is, but I don't like him.

"If I cleaned it, it wouldn't look like shit, now would it?" she asks sensibly.

"I thought you were gonna clean it."

"Tomorrow."

"What'd you do today?" he asks.

"Survived," she shoots back.

"You don't have to be an asshole, I was just asking a question," he tells her.

I already want to punch this guy in the goddamn face.

"It's the anniversary of my dad dying," she states. "I did what I always do."

"Oh." He pauses, and I hope he feels like a douchebag. "I'm sorry."

"Thanks."

Her voice is so…unlike what I'd heard in the few minutes I'd been with her. Robotic.

Guy clears his throat. "You never did tell me what that was, you know."

"I know."

He waits. "So, you wanna tell me what it is you do? I always wondered."

"I'm going to take a shower," she says, as if he hadn't spoken.

And then there's silence. I hear what I assume is the bathroom door closing, then him mutter, "Fucking cunt," and I'm tempted to turn the amplifier off.

A few minutes later the side door slams shut and a skinny dude with a cigarette hanging out of his mouth and a limp brown ponytail steps into the driveway. He drops an empty milk jug into a bin by the door and gets in his truck. I watch as it backs out and debate abandoning my post so I can follow the little weasel.

But I stay put.

I wait—and swat off fantasies—while she showers and remain where I'm at for the rest of the evening. Even after it seems like she's gone to bed, I still wait.

I'm not sure what I'm waiting for until the male returns, nearing 2:30 am. I was sort of napping in my seat with a hell of a sore neck when he came weaving up the road. He took the corner of his driveway too fast and knocked over the empty garbage can by the edge of the road.

He's muttering as he climbs out of the car, but he hauls his drunk ass to the end of the driveway to retrieve the garbage can. By the time he makes it back in the house, I have a bad feeling. Nothing too ominous, nothing relating to my job, but a hunch about the nature of their relationship that leaves a bad taste in my mouth.

I turn the amplifier back up and listen to his drunken fumbling for a few minutes. I eye up the windows. I already pinpointed her bedroom when she went into it. Against the interest of stealth, I drop the amplifier and creep up the driveway, alongside the house and around to the back where the bedroom is. Like the living room, it has more windows than it should. I find a good one and peer inside.

The drunk asshole is climbing into bed with her. I feel like I should leave, but I stay. This is not what I was assigned to do. This has nothing to do with the mission. What's more, I don't want to see it.

Her back is to him when he climbs in, her eyes closed. She doesn't look peaceful, exactly, more like… determined?

He rolls over and starts pawing at her. His hand closes over her breast and her eyes open, not a trace of surprise, like she'd just woken up, but her lip curls up faintly in disgust. When he doesn't stop pawing, she finally lets him know she's awake and pushes his hand off her, pointedly giving him her shoulder.

It looks like he says something, but it's quiet and I don't have the amplifier so I don't know what.

She says something back and closes her eyes.

He reaches over again and the scene unfolds just like before. Three more times before he gets pissed. He's drunk and stumbling but he throws back the blanket and comes out of bed, whipping the blanket off her and throwing it on the floor. I watch her grit her teeth and visibly seethe, but he can't see with her back to him. She closes her eyes again, as if unbothered.

But then the douchebag crosses to her side of the bed. I look to the door, guessing at the floorplan. It wouldn't take me long to get through the front door, even if it's locked. A few seconds to get to the bedroom.

Douchebag pounces on her and it's the scariest fucking ten seconds of my day as I watch her struggle with him, kicking and scratching and finally throwing the motherfucker off the bed and onto the floor where he belongs.

Popping up, he screams at her, and I don't need an amplifier to hear, "Some fucking wife you are!"

"Go to hell," she says back, loudly enough for me to hear.

"What the fuck do you want me to do, huh?" he demands.

"Why don't you go back to one of your dumb fucking whores?" she suggests, and though it's loud enough I understand what she's saying, she's not screaming. And… she's smiling.

"You'd love that, wouldn't you? You'd fucking love that." He's still screaming. He's still pissed. Flinging his arms around. Acting a fool.

"I would," she tells him. "I *would* fucking love that. Stay all night. She can make you breakfast."

"You fucking jealous?"

She literally laughs. Not an angry, bitter laugh, but like he actually told a joke.

That infuriates him more and he whirls around, throwing his fist into the wall.

She's no longer laughing, but watching soberly to see what he'll do next.

"You're a fucking psycho," he spits at her as he storms out of the room.

She seems to wait until she hears a door slam, then she gets up and retrieves the blanket from the floor. She drapes it back over the bed and then climbs right up in the middle.

I'm about to wait for him to come back and see there's no room in the bed for him, but then I hear him outside. I lean away from the window and back up against the house. I'm sure he's heading to his truck, but I brace myself to attack just in case.

The engine roars to life and his tires crunch the rocks beneath them as he rolls out of the driveway. He shouldn't be driving, but I'm just glad he left the house, to be honest.

I peek into her room one more time but she's back in bed, seemingly asleep. She's curled up in the fetal position with her blanket around her and this time she looks peaceful.

Mission accomplished, I hustle back to my car and head in the direction I just saw her husband go. Partially I want to make sure he doesn't cause any accidents, but mostly I want to see where he's going.

I follow him to another shitty little house on another shitty little corner. The porch light is on and he stumbles up to the stoop. Door opens and a chubby brunette stands there with her arms crossed at first, but then he throws his arms around her and gives her a desperate bear hug and she softens, securing her arms around him and hugging him back.

He follows her inside and the porch light goes off.

Shaking my head in disgust, I turn around and head back to Brooklyn. I'm not sure yet what I'm going to tell Raj, because I don't want to tell him what I've seen. I'm so disgusted by all of it, I can only imagine what *she* feels.

I try to shut down my interest in the life of Annabelle Whatever Her Last Name Is, but I find myself hoping I get assigned to keep an eye on her again.

CHAPTER THREE
Annabelle

I carry all the grocery bags in one trip, even though the weight makes the plastic stretch thin and cut the circulation off in my fingers. I would sort of rather lose a finger than have to spend even one more minute at my mother's house.

Well, Pietro's house.

It used to be my home, long ago, but it's nothing like that now.

By the time I make it to the kitchen, I can't feel the tips of two fingers. I drop the bags on the countertop and look at my hand, squeezing the numb tips.

"Can you cut up the potatoes?"

My shoulders droop. "I can't stay, Ma, I told you."

"It'll take you two minutes," she says, rolling her eyes and turning her back to me.

Which is like four hours here, but arguing will only take longer. I grab a knife and a cutting board and start slicing potatoes in half.

"Don't forget to wash them," she tells me, stopping what

she's doing to watch me. Pretty sure it defeats the time-saving purpose of me cutting them in the first place, but what do I know?

I say nothing, plopping the halved potato under some water.

Satisfied, she rifles through the bags, making the odd comment that I ignore completely.

I ignore people a lot. It's just easier. They annoy me and I don't want to deal with it, so I act like I don't hear them. Paul actually tells his associates (friends?) that I'm deaf in one ear, to explain why sometimes I blatantly ignore him even in front of them. If anyone notices that it doesn't matter which side he's on, no one mentions it.

"How's your depression?" pierces my veil of ignoring.

I roll my eyes, because fucking fuck.

"I'm not fucking depressed."

"Watch your language!" she says, eyes widening as if a pew of churchgoers are watching us prepare dinner.

It's Pietro. My goddamn stepfather told my mom I'm depressed. I'm not depressed. I'm miserable. There's a huge difference. My problem is not in my brain, it's my actual life.

"You should spend more time with your family," she tells me.

Now *that* would depress me.

"You were $2 short, by the way," I tell her. I had no problem going to the store and getting her groceries, but I couldn't afford to pay for any myself.

"I'll give it to you before you leave."

I really wanted that to be like 30 seconds ago, but I just slice another potato.

"Why didn't you get the baby carrots?" she asks, pulling out the bag of full-size carrots and holding them up by the corner like a bag of soggy waffles.

"They were out of the ones on sale. Those were cheaper."

"Well, you'll have to chop them up," she tells me, tossing the disappointing carrots on the counter next to me.

I chop the next potato a little more enthusiastically and hold it under the water. "When does he get home?"

I never mention his name if I can help it, like he's Voldemort.

"Oh, I don't know," she says, hand fluttering. She takes a seat at the table and begins leafing through a magazine. "Cut the carrots up the size of baby carrots. Petey doesn't like his carrots to be that thick. If you get a really thick one, slice it in half."

My eyes narrow and I bite back some lewd remarks. I just wanna get out of here, so I cut the last potato and set to work on the carrots.

By the time all is said and done, I've completely prepped the vegetables for her roast and chopped the tops off her bell peppers for the appetizer. Before she can find enough for me to do so I'll be there to put everything in—and maybe serve it for them, if I can find a nice maid's costume—I tell her I have to go, that Paul's expecting me.

"Tell him I say hi, and you're welcome to come for dinner. Your brother and sister have been asking to see you."

"I already have dinner on," I lie. Because it's an old habit that she never let me break even after my desire to do it had long died, I go over and kiss her on the cheek before I make my break for the door.

Only after I get to the car do I realize I forgot to get the money she owed me for her groceries.

Oh well, it's not worth going back in to get it.

The dinner I lied about earlier being, well, a lie, I slide a frozen pizza into the oven a half hour before Paul's supposed to be home. I actually can cook, I actually *like* to cook, but Paul enjoys it so much that I seldom do it. The last thing I want to do is make my husband happy.

Turns out I could've that night, since Paul didn't come home when he was supposed to.

Or at all.

The following day he isn't home either. I consider shooting him a text to see if he's alive, but I don't care enough to type it out. Mostly I just want to know if I'll have the bed to myself again, because I love having the bed to myself.

By afternoon I still haven't heard from him so I decide, fuck it, I'm gonna make myself a nice dinner. I never did get that money from my mom and I probably shouldn't splurge on extra groceries since Paul hasn't been bringing much home lately, but I do it anyway. I buy myself a nice—cheap—bottle of wine and all the ingredients to make my famous chicken parm. I'm literally humming as I stroll out of the grocery store, so excited for the night ahead of me.

I pour myself a glass and turn on some music while I prepare it, swaying around the tiny kitchen, using my sink as a makeshift counter since there's not enough room for all the dishes.

I hate this goddamn house and its stupid, tiny kitchen.

But I'm so excited to eat that I can't even be bothered. Plus I'm on my second glass of wine, and the world gets pretty rosy when I'm on my second glass of wine.

My thoughts, fueled by wine, drift back to the mean, sexy

guard back at the old junkyard. *Liam*. What a sexy name. He has to be sexy with the name Liam, right?

"Liam," I murmur it aloud, just to hear it on my lips. Sounds nice. Like his shoulders. I've always been a sucker for a man with broad, strong shoulders.

Paul has such lame, disappointing shoulders. Hate Paul. Not gonna think about Paul.

Liam, sexy Liam. With his sexy hips all pressed against mine.

I mean, sure, in real life he's probably a bully asshole like all the rest, but safely tucked away in Fantasyland, I'll pretend he's just kinky.

I giggle to myself and pour another glass of wine.

I don't even get two sips in when I hear Paul's truck pull into the drive.

"Oh no!" In my tipsy state, this seems like a bigger crisis than it is. I want all the chicken parm for myself. I don't want Paul to know I even remember how to make chicken parm, because then he'll start pestering me to cook again.

I contemplate dramatically ripping it from the oven and throwing it in the trash before he can make it inside, because hate Paul—but I don't, because love chicken parm.

"Oh well," I finally say, more mournfully than is justifiable, really, but fuck it, more wine.

Life is good!

The door opens and life gets less good, even with wine, but I suck down a few more gulps, trying to hold onto my happiness.

"Damn, that smells good," Paul says as he steps inside.

Stupid Paul and his stupid long nose, smelling the food I cooked. He doesn't deserve to smell the food I cooked.

I ignore him.

The fleeting thought that I should reinforce him saying nice things crosses my mind, but I strike it down, because of the whole "fuck it" thing.

I gulp more wine.

Too much wine, too fast, and I'm really starting to feel it. I place a stabilizing hand on the edge of the counter and blink hard a few times.

"What's the occasion?" he asks, since I cooked.

"I didn't think you'd be home," I answer honestly, and with an earnest grin on my face.

Any trace of cheer on his face drains at the jab, and that's when I notice he has a black eye.

"What happened to your face?" I ask without tact.

He grows even surlier. "Some stupid motherfucker doesn't know who he's dealing with, that's what," he mutters.

That sounds boring, so I nod and walk away to the other room.

Well, I try, but walking is hard. Eventually I make it to the bedroom, kick the door closed, and collapse on my bed, feeling a bit weightless. The room feels spinny, but it's not *actually* spinning, so I'm not afraid I'll throw up. Everything just feels light and wonderful, and I wonder why I don't get drunk every day. Life would be so much easier to handle.

"Ah, right," I say, to absolutely no one. "I can't afford to!"

Maybe I should be nice to my mom and Pietro to get some money.

Nope. Not worth it. Even drunk, that's absurd.

The door creaks open and I sigh, put upon. Even though he's close, I hear myself saying very loudly, "You should buy me more wine!"

"Why?"

"Because I love wine. Wine makes me happy."

"Maybe your *husband* would if you'd be less of a bitch every day."

"You're not my husband," I inform him.

He doesn't speak, but he doesn't have to. That's the unspeakable, and I've consumed enough alcohol to say it.

He crosses the room in what seems like one angry stride and lifts me off the bed, but it isn't sexy when he does it. He's not powerful, he's not strong, and he tries to hurt me, digging his bony fucking fingers into my shoulder as he shoves me across the room.

"What'd you fucking say?"

"You fucking heard me," I say, and swat away the next hand that comes my way. He pushes me back against the wall, but with his pathetic little hands, not with his body, and I don't want his body anywhere near mine anyway.

I can see in his face he wants to hit me, but I just smile, like I don't have a care in the world. "Go ahead, motherfucker. Hit me in the face. You're *so* big and strong, you can harm little ol' me. Go on!"

But he doesn't. I have no idea why. Normally he would. Probably not the face, but my arms, my chest, my sides, the softness of my abdomen where he could make me double over and feel like vomiting.

He just shakes his head, looking like he hates me every bit as much as I hate him. "Fuck you," he says instead.

"Never," I throw back, still smiling.

That pisses him off more and I see the fist coming at me. Despite myself, I flinch, try to duck away from it, but it doesn't connect with my face or my arm, it connects with the wall behind my head.

"I hate coming home to you!" he screams.

"So *stop doing it*," I scream back, wanting to rip my long, dark hair out right at the roots. "For the love of God, you have to know I don't want you here! Why can't you just stay with someone else? Won't you be happier?"

I'm not even being mean at this point, the alcohol is just compelling me to sheer honesty, and it pisses him off like I'm throwing jabs. He storms out of the bedroom and down the hall, cursing and hitting walls.

He's gonna kill me someday.

Sober, that might actually scare me, but I'm drunk and I don't care.

If I cared, I probably wouldn't have snuck past two armed men to steal a couple of goddamn apples.

Suddenly exhausted, I climb into bed and curl up with my blanket cocoon. I dreamed last night that my dad was still alive and I went to stay with him. Paul existed somewhere in the world, but he wasn't my cross to bear anymore. I made dinner for me and my dad and we sat at our old dining room table and ate Grandma's spaghetti while we talked. There were apples in a fruit bowl between us.

Tears well in my eyes and I hate them.

I pull the blanket up over my head, because I just can't handle the world anymore today.

CHAPTER FOUR
Annabelle

I have no memory of getting out of bed at any point during the night and getting my chicken parm out of the oven, let alone turning the oven off and putting the untouched chicken parm in a container and into my fridge. I spend about ten minutes walking through my kitchen, head cloudy, trying to figure out how this could have happened. I consider that Paul could've done it, but that's ridiculous. I know he left; he wouldn't have come back to do that, wouldn't have even known I didn't take it out myself. And if he would've, he would've eaten some.

I take the container out of the fridge and lift the lid. Actually, it does look like someone ripped off a bottom piece, but it probably just stuck to the pan and my drunken, apparently sleepwalking self didn't care.

I toss the bowl on the counter, because I'm starving, and now I have lunch.

When I grab a plate for my lunch, I realize the sink is empty.

I mean, I had it empty when I put the chicken in the oven, but the pan I'd cooked it in should be in there, courtesy of Drunk

Annabelle.

It's not. It's clean and dry in the strainer beside my sink. I washed it?

Since I went to bed so early last night, I'm up a little earlier than I planned to be. I'm not hungover, but I'm definitely foggy. I look for my wine where I'd left it on the counter, but I find it with the top back on in the refrigerator.

Did I really drink enough to black out?

God.

I shudder, thankful—hoping—that Paul *didn't* come back last night. He could've done anything to me and I wouldn't even know.

"Maybe we'll cut you off at two glasses next time," I tell the wine as I slide the remaining portion of chicken parm back in the fridge for later.

I wish I could change the locks, but it's his house. He might actually combust if he came back to changed locks. A girl can dream.

I feel a little on the gross side though, so after lunch I shower and spend the day doing laundry. I clean all the bedding so it doesn't smell like a wine factory and vacuum all the carpeted floors. I don't feel like cleaning the wood floors, so I don't.

This house was such a wreck when we first got it. Paul hadn't believed me when I assured him we could make it nice without spending a fortune, but I saw the potential.

In the house, not in him. I'm not *crazy*.

And I did make it nice, piece by piece, room by room. But it was still his, so it could never be mine, so I couldn't really even find any pride in the accomplishment.

One more task off the to-do list. Sometimes my whole life feels like a to-do list, and I'm just waiting until I finish it all so I can take that final dirt nap.

The phone rings, pulling me from my delightfully morbid thoughts.

It's my mother on the other end. "What are you doing?"

"Fixing to wash the lunch dishes. Why?"

"I need you to come with me to pick up my dress for the party."

"No."

She pauses, like she didn't hear me. "Huh?"

"No."

The 10 year anniversary of my father's death has barely passed, and she's buying a dress for her 10 year wedding anniversary. Because my mother remarried with her husband's body barely cool in the ground.

To the bastard responsible for killing him, but let's not even go there right now, because wine fog.

"I can't."

Not entirely accurate. More like "I won't," but in that, my foot was going down.

"Come on," she whines. "I wanna buy you a new dress, too."

I feel like a faithless, sellout bastard for even agreeing to attend the party. "I don't need a new dress. I have dresses."

"I'll kill you if you wear black," she states, because she knows me.

I smile at the idea, but say nothing.

"Annabelle, I'm serious."

I finally tell her I'll go dress shopping with her one day next week, just to get her off my back—and off the phone.

I didn't always dislike my mother, of course. Once upon a time we'd been closer. When I was little, we were even *close*, no r needed. When my father was alive and we were a family and everything was fine. Before I knew the atrocities of the world I'd been born into, before she married one of them.

Not anymore. Too much damage has been done and I don't even desire to resuscitate the relationship at this point.

She betrayed my father and ruined my life.

She'll never admit she did.

We're at an impasse.

The day passes in a fog. I get a lot done around the house early on, then I'm exhausted and I crash in the afternoon. I accomplish nothing more. I don't put a pizza in the oven or consider calling to have one delivered. I don't warm up chicken parm. I don't do anything. I stay in bed, wrapped up in my blanket cocoon, because that's the only safe place in the world.

I don't even know if he'll come home tonight. He probably won't. Usually when we have a big blowout, he stays gone overnight. Well, if he has a girlfriend who will put up with that. The one he has now seems like a real dipshit; she's put up with all of his crap—and my existence—for a year now. I can't imagine a woman *wanting* him, let alone enough to deal with all that, but to each her own. As long as she does her job and keeps the bastard busy, she's fine by me.

Apparently not, however, as come evening I hear his truck pull up. Either it's getting louder or I'm dramatizing it in my head, but I'm pretty sure it's getting louder. Probably needs fixing. I'd like to take it to someone legit, but it's not in the budget, so I'll tell him to take it to one of his chop shop guys.

"I know," he'll whine, like he'd already thought of it and arranged it and God, why did I have to be so overbearing?

"Ugh," I mutter, already dreading his company and he's not even through the front door.

Maybe I'll leave. It's not too cold out, and surely I could find something to do. I eye up my camera, sitting in the corner, abandoned. I used to love to go out and take photographs, but I don't find much joy in it anymore, so it's been a while since I've picked it up.

The thought makes me sad, so I curl up in my blankets.

I expect him to come in, but a long stretch passes and he doesn't. I relax a little. The room remains still, unbothered by him. I can almost imagine he's not here, except I can hear the television on in the living room—and I never have it on.

While he curls up on the couch alone, I curl up with my fantasies. Wild fantasies, like, wouldn't it be wonderful if I could call the cops and report him? I wonder how long I would get to feel free before Pietro's people would take me out and make it all go away, not wanting the cops to have a chance to talk to him.

Wilder fantasies. Liam floats into my head, even though I'm sober. I imagine him kidnapping me, because, I don't know, I discovered whatever the hell they were doing at the old shop. He doesn't want to hurt me though. Neither does Raj, he just doesn't know what to do with me. Liam volunteers to keep me with him until they can trust that I'm on their side. Sexy times ensue.

I sigh, my hand lazily moving across my breast. I'd like to get myself off, but I won't take the chance with Paul in the house.

No one's going to kidnap me away from the stupid lout.

I can't call the police.

I'm trapped, and there's no way out, only ways to dig in

deeper. My mom's pissed she doesn't have grandkids yet, but I imagine she'd be a shit grandmother anyway. On the surface she wouldn't—she'd buy them presents and fuss over them to all her friends, but if it ever came down to it and they really needed her, she wouldn't be there. That's her way.

And, well, fuck that.

Bringing anyone into Pietro's world is nothing short of a travesty anyway. We're all pawns—meaningless, unloved pawns, and no one deserves to live like that.

Feeling worse than I did before, I can't find the motivation to get out of bed. I do sort of have to pee, but I'm not convinced it's worth it.

Instead I close my eyes and go to my safe place, free of thoughts if my subconscious is feeling particularly kind tonight.

I jolt awake.

It's dark and my head pounds, and for a disorienting moment, I'm not sure what woke me.

"You gonna sleep all day?"

Dread swallows me up like gooey, slow-moving quicksand.

I smell alcohol, and I cleaned the bedding so it's not from me. He's hovering over my shoulder, head bobbing. I can feel his breath on my right bicep, and it makes me want to cut my arm off.

"It's dark," I mutter, gravelly. Why would you wake a person up like that during the actual night? Maybe he *is* the devil.

"You've been sleepin' all damn day," he says, slurring his words enough to make me tense up.

I haven't slept all day, I cleaned this morning, but I don't argue.

"Just leave me alone," I say, wrapping my blanket tighter.

He grabs it before I can tuck it beneath me, fisting it in his hands. He's figured out my blankets are my safety, so he loves to rip them off me. I always end up letting go, simply because I know we can't afford to replace them if they tear.

I hate letting him win, but sometimes you have to lose the battle to win the war.

Thing is, I'm tired and I don't feel like fighting. I let him yank the blanket off me. I even roll over since he can't pull the part that's wedged under my body.

"These fucking blankets," he mutters.

I say nothing. I close my eyes and try to mentally fend off what I know is coming. I get so tired of fighting. He leaves me alone, except when he drinks. Lately he drinks a lot more than he used to, and he's draining me. I don't know how much more I can take. I don't know how much more he can take. We're engaged in a deadly game of chicken, and one of us is going to lose big soon, I can feel it.

Probably me.

Termites like him always find a way to make it on to the next beautiful house, so they can eat away at its insides until it fucking crumbles.

I do fight though. I always fight, even if I don't have the energy. I *don't* have the energy to smile or laugh or try to make him feel like shit. I wish I did, but I don't.

His hands are on me in a flash, knowing he's in for a fight. He can't move slow, like a lover, because he isn't my lover, and I don't want him. He knows, I know, so it can't be like that, it has to be a fight.

I don't think I have the energy to win tonight. I usually win, but this time I anticipate a loss.

He's especially pissed tonight. I've been grating on his pathetic pride all week, and the incident with the wine was really bad. I said the thing that makes him angriest; I never pull that one out, regardless of how bitchy I am to him, because I don't want to piss him off to the point he might be out for my actual blood. But I did, so I should've known this was coming. This is how he knows he can inflict pain, even if I feign otherwise.

I try fighting but my arms are pinned down painfully. Not sexy. I buck and twist, try to get my knee up, but he mounted me in just the right position and none of it's working.

He's fumbling with his pajama pants. I turn my face away in disgust. At least he can't make me watch.

I manage to jerk my hands free again while he fumbles but he lunges, recapturing them before I can even push him off. To punish my attempt, he crushes his thin, gross body against me and tries to kiss me. Not with tongue, since he knows I will legitimately fucking bite it off.

My skin crawls. His fingernails bite into my wrists. I close my eyes and jerk my head away from his disgusting breath and his smarmy little lips. I can feel the hand he freed up working to push himself between my clenched legs. He pinches me, shoves me. I know there will be bruises on my thighs tomorrow.

And then suddenly, his weight is gone. He isn't crushing me—my arms are free.

I hear a crash, a grunt, a yelp.

Did he fall off the bed?

I'm confused—and a little scared—but I open my eyes to see what's going on.

I jump, scurrying up the bed, trying to cover myself with my nightie.

Paul is sprawled in the floor, mouth bloody, and a muddy black boot rests across his neck. I can't believe my eyes as I follow the trail up from his boot. I have to be dreaming. Why would *he* be *here*?

Liam from the junkyard is standing in my bedroom, muscles bathed in moonlight, with his boot across Paul's throat. He leans forward, putting a little more weight on it. Paul flails. He's crying—actually crying. I cover my mouth, because I want to laugh, I really do. I wonder if he's pissed himself.

As attracted to Liam as I was on sight, right now? Right now he's a goddamn superhero.

Liam spares me a glance over his shoulder and my heart pounds so hard, I think we must all hear it.

"You okay?" he asks.

I nod, eyes wide, without words.

A little more pressure, and I wonder if he might kill Paul. I'm curious, but by no means concerned. Maybe he has people who could clean that up. If not, maybe I could help him. He's pretty strong, he could drag Paul's body out of here. I'll just tell Pietro's guys Paul never came home from his girlfriend's house.

Liam hunches over so he can look Paul in the face. His stoicism might be even more terrifying than anger, and he's completely calm when he says, "You ever lay an unwelcome hand on her again, and I'll kill you." He presses his boot down even harder. "Understand?"

Tears streaming down his face, Paul tries to nod. Liam lets up, stepping off to the side, and Paul climbs shakily to his hands and knees, spittle and snot dripping from his long, pathetic face. He sits back on his knees and holds his throat, making pitiful little noises.

The contrast between his wretched hunched form and Liam standing tall beside him is emblazoned in my fantasies forever.

I meet Liam's gaze and hold it for a moment, but neither of us says anything.

Without sparing Paul another glance, Liam turns and barges right out of my life.

CHAPTER FIVE
Liam

I'm on guard duty with Lance when I see her coming down the road.

I'd been watching for her all morning, just on the off chance she came. I thought she might, against Raj's warning and common sense, but I hoped she wouldn't.

I knew I shouldn't have interfered last night, but I couldn't stop myself. I couldn't do nothing. I'd be as bad as her sniveling little shitbag husband.

But doing something had consequences, too.

For both of us.

"Stay here," I tell Lance, propping my gun up against the fence.

He goes alert, eager for conflict. "What? What do you see?"

"Don't worry about it, just stay here," I tell him before taking off toward the road.

She slows to a stop, her gaze moving warily to Lance.

In lieu of a greeting, I say, "You shouldn't be here."

"So I've heard." She shifts her weight, as if unsure. She's

holding a wrapped cloth, and without warning or explanation she thrusts it in my direction.

It's barely warm since she had to travel so long to get here, but a whiff and a look tells me it might be an apple turnover. My mouth waters, but I don't betray any sort of pleasure.

"What's this?" I ask evenly.

Her cheeks are a little flushed, and I don't know if it's from the cool autumn air or me being a jackass. I hope it's the former, but it's probably the latter.

She shrugs, self-conscious. "I had extra."

I sigh, glancing back at Lance to make sure he's still where I left him.

"You can't come here," I tell her.

"Why?"

I look back at her. "You just can't. Raj told you to stay away."

She knows that, and she glances at Lance, too. "I don't care what they're doing in there."

She would if she knew what that was, but I say nothing.

Now she's looking back at me, her big brown eyes faintly imploring. "Why were you at my house last night?"

I avert my gaze. I'm not sure how to explain that. I shouldn't have been there, and the truth is, I don't know why I was. I settle on a half-truth. "Raj told me to follow you home the day you left. Make sure you weren't spying for your stepfather."

Her nose wrinkles up at the mention of him. "Ew. Why would I ever do that?"

I raise my eyebrows, since that should be obvious.

Annabelle shakes her head. "I hate him. I would never help him with anything. I wouldn't piss on him if he was on fire."

It's funny she should say that. I've stalked her enough to

know she isn't spying, but I'm curious at her level of hatred for the man. I mean, he's very hateable, and most people do feel that way, but they still fear him enough to do his bidding. And she's family.

Well, sort of.

Miss De Luca-Covello.

Or Mrs., I should say.

The reminder that she's married effectively cools me down.

"You need to leave. Lance is a bulldog, he could go in and tell Raj you're here any second."

"Raj always liked me," she says, glancing at the old building.

"Raj still doesn't believe your loyalties don't lie with Pietro."

That makes her smile for some reason.

"Maybe instead of following me, you should kidnap me until he can be convinced I'm on your side," she advises, flashing me a smile. Her brown eyes are warm as she looks at me, like I'm a goddamn knight in shining armor instead of the guy she now knows has been stalking her. Girl's ten kinds of crazy, but damn, is she pretty.

Since it gives me the opening to bring it up though, I find I can't pass it up. "I think your husband might notice you missing."

Her eyes go dim at that and her whole face seems to darken. I feel like an asshole, but remind myself, hey, she's the one who married the guy.

I wish I could tell her I'd help her if she wanted to leave him. I wish there was any point.

I feel bad for her, and I wish I didn't know what I know.

She deserves more.

I want to know things I shouldn't care about. Things I *can't* care about.

Then she says, "He's not my husband."

That's confusing, and I frown. "He seems to think he is."

Annabelle looks aggravated and shakes her head. "He isn't. Not really."

"Then what the hell is he?"

"I feel like you should buy me a drink before I get into all that," she sort of jokes, kicking at a spot on the ground with a cute little smile.

That's exactly the kind of thing I shouldn't do, but I can't keep standing here and she doesn't seem inclined to listen to me when I tell her to go away.

"All right," I say, formulating a new plan on the fly. "Is there somewhere near your house we could go to get one?"

Grimacing, she said, "Paul's a regular at most of the bars."

"Food?"

She pauses. "There's a deli up the road."

I remember it. I nod. "I know the place. I'll meet you there tonight."

"When?" Her eyes light with excitement and I feel both encouraged and apprehensive.

"Seven." I miss half a beat. "Now, I need you to wipe that look off your face and look like I just pissed you off, let you down easy, but you didn't take it well."

She narrows her eyes as if annoyed, but there's a trace of amusement there. "Really? I doubt you're *that* good."

I'm amused, but I don't show it. "Just listen to me for once, huh?"

She nods too quickly, her lips pursing, like she just greeted me wearing Saran wrap and I didn't even look. "All right. Fine. Be that way."

I bite back a smile. Lance can't see my face, but I don't want to test her composure.

Then I reach out and pat her on the arm with a, "you'll be okay."

"Oh my God, I hate you," she says, barely holding on. "Later I want the phone numbers of everyone you've ever dumped so I can personally apologize on your behalf."

I don't smile with my mouth, but I wink at her before I turn and head back to my post. As I do, I'm hit with a troubling flicker of excitement at the prospect of seeing her again, face-to-face.

My amusement quickly fades and I don't look at Lance as I approach. I retrieve my gun and resume my position, tossing him a half smile and saying, "Thanks."

He's frowning. Always suspicious. Always assuming the worst. I understand the impulse, but it's damned annoying when you're on this side.

"What was that all about?" he asks, guarded.

I'm still not sure this is the best strategy, but it *is* the best way to make it clear she's not special, I don't care about her, and I'm damn sure not going to put my ass on the line for her.

"I fucked her," I tell him simply.

The furrowing between his brow subsides and his bro-side wins out. "Aw, shit. She caught feelings?"

I shrug, like I collect one night stands. "Sometimes it happens. Can't be helped."

"Her though?" He shakes his head. "Damn, man."

"I know, I know." I smile a little self-deprecatingly. "Least we don't have to worry about her coming around here again. Pretty sure she'd be too embarrassed."

"How was she?" he asks, because he's Lance.

I shrug as if unimpressed. "Eh."

He laughs, delighted, also because he's Lance.

He nods at the wrapped parcel in my hand, the one I'd forgotten about, preoccupied with coming up with a reason for her showing up. "What's that?"

"Oh." I look down at it, frown. "Apple turnover or something? I wasn't totally listening."

That's a lie, but Lance is still pleased. His mother must not have loved him.

I unwrap it and take a whiff. My mouth waters and I take a big old bite out of it.

Lance is shaking his head, smiling. "You're cold, man."

I grin and take another bite.

CHAPTER SIX
Annabelle

My nerves are eating me alive. I've changed clothes five times and I feel ridiculous. I've never seen Liam in anything but his gear, and I don't even know if he'll still be wearing it. I feel stupid, but I've never actually been on a date before.

Well, not that this is a date.

Or is it? I don't even know. I just know I want to do better than jeans and a bulky sweater, which—aside from my disheveled nightie in the moonlight—is all he's ever seen me in.

By the time I arrive at the deli, you can't tell I changed clothes seven times or rummaged like hell through drawers looking for something that passed for a matching bra and panty set. I'm cool and collected as I wait for him by the door.

He gets there right at seven.

He's still in a stripped down version of his gear—a fitted black t-shirt and his usual dark camo pants. He looks really good. I'm convinced he would look good in a sparkly pink tutu, but a tight black shirt that hugs his bulging biceps and hints at the chiseled physique beneath? Yes, please.

I found a red long-sleeved top with peek-a-boo shoulder

cutouts in my closet. I don't recall ever buying it, but my mom probably gave it to me for Christmas one year. I paired it with this fabulous bra she got that has zigzagging straps across the chest, and a pair of snug jeans. I even curled my hair. I feel a lot sexier than I have, maybe ever, which seems like a good place to start a maybe-date.

When Liam sees me, he rakes an appreciative gaze over my ensemble and moves in closer. He smells good and I already want to kiss him. It's not my style, but I'd skip the sandwiches and go home with him now if he asked.

He places a hand at the small of my back to guide me toward the line, but I suspect it's just an excuse to touch me. Boy, am I fine with that.

"How are you?" he asks.

"Good," I answer brightly. "How was… work?"

I watch his mouth tug up ever so slightly in amusement, but he doesn't fully smile. "Not too bad. This crazy girl showed up though, kind of threw a wrench in things."

"Oh yeah? Was she hot?" I take a step forward, waiting for Marco to approach the counter and take our order.

He finally looks at me, but settles on cutting me a look of disapproval, then pointedly looking at Liam, then walking away.

Oops.

"She was," he says, placing his hands on my hips and pulling me in front of him. He pulls me against his hard body and wraps his arms around me in a sort of crisscross embrace, then calls over, "We're ready to order."

He must've noticed Marco giving me the stink eye. I'm as red as my shirt at this point, and so is Marco, which is more impressive given his darker complexion.

He takes our order but he doesn't like it. I can't see the look

Liam is giving him, but I pick up on his controlled tone and the unhappy but obedient motions Marco makes as he goes about taking our order, so I assume Liam is alpha-dogging him.

Poor Marco. He doesn't know Paul isn't my real husband. I'll have to make him a strudel or something.

Once his point's made, Liam releases me and my chest feels inexplicably empty. I want him to do that again. No one's ever embraced me that way before and I like it.

Liam pays and carries the tray with both of our sandwiches over to a table. He doesn't ask where I want to sit, and I like his casual dominance.

Once we're seated, I'm not entirely sure what to do. He distributes our sandwiches and I murmur a thank you, then there's a moment where I'm more preoccupied than I should be with a sandwich. I eye the glob of mayonnaise slinking down the side of my bun. I wonder why I picked something so potentially messy for the first time we ever share a meal together.

I wonder why I say that like there will be many more times.

I wonder where this could possibly go.

I wonder if he's thinking any of that.

Finally, I try to stop thinking and focus on the sandwich again. I steal a glance at Liam without lifting my head and drawing his attention.

He's moving the top bun and looking at the stack of meat beneath like it's disappointed him. I hope he never looks at me like that.

I'm getting ahead of myself again. Way ahead of myself.

Dropping the bun back on top of his sandwich, Liam reaches beneath the table and draws two beer bottles out of the many pockets of his pants.

I laugh as he uncaps one and hands it to me, and he cracks a smile.

"Thank you," I say, while glancing uncertainly behind the counter at Marco. "I'm pretty sure this isn't allowed though."

"Then he can say something to me about it."

One look at his size, stoicism, and general ooze of intimidation gets his point across—he's not going to.

I've been in the company of dangerous men my entire life, so I don't know why he feels so much more impressive. Using that strength and intimidation to protect *me* probably helps. Normally they're not doing that.

I don't know *why* he protected me, but it gives me the boost of confidence I need to ask. I take a sip of the beer he just handed me first, then I dive right in. "So, why were you outside my house last night?"

He rotates his beer on the tabletop, studying it. "I told you, Raj had me follow you."

"Was someone else following me while you were at work?"

"No."

"Then what's the point? I could've engaged in all sorts of deviance while you were guarding the junkyard."

"You weren't," he says, apparently unconcerned.

He didn't answer my question, at least not honestly, so I lift my eyebrows expectantly.

"What?" he asks.

"If you want me to answer your questions, you should probably answer mine."

"What makes you think I care if you answer my questions?" he shoots back.

I flush, but hold my ground. "You're here, aren't you?"

He sits back in his seat and sighs. "I only *had* to follow you that first night."

"But you kept doing it?"

He shrugs, half sheepish, half, "Well, yeah."

"Why?" I ask.

At first he doesn't answer, then he fingers the discarded cap of his beer bottle, watching it instead of me. "It didn't seem like you were safe."

My insides melt. "Well... I'm glad you did."

He nods, seeming uncomfortable.

I nod as well, looking at my sandwich. I'm hungry, but I feel weird eating if he's not going to. "I know he's not much, but Paul does have dirty friends, associates, people who... would do stuff for him. I immensely appreciate what you did, but—"

He holds up a large hand to stop me. "If any variation of you telling me to watch out for the retaliation of that little weasel is about to come out of your mouth, don't."

"I'm sure you can look out for yourself," I say, trying to take the sting out of the hit I must've dealt his ego. "It's just, I would feel really terrible if you got hurt for defending me. It's not like it would be a fair fight. Obviously *Paul* can't hurt you, but...."

"I'm not afraid of your husband."

He's immovable and I drop it because I really wasn't trying to offend him.

Since I don't respond, he folds his arms across his chest and says, "Speaking of, you were supposed to explain how he's not really your husband."

I grab my beer and give it a shake. "You were supposed to wait until I had a little more of this."

He smiles as I take a sip, but waits for my answer.

I take another long sip, snippets of my farce of a wedding playing across my mind. Father McCarthy's wrinkled brow dripping sweat as I stood at the altar wordlessly. The threatening glares of Pietro's goons, the man himself seated calmly beside my mother in the family pew, knowing his will would be done regardless.

"I never consented to it," I finally tell him. "I never spoke the words, never signed a paper. I wanted no part of it. It just didn't matter."

"How do you get married without saying a word?" he asks.

I shrug. "It was a small ceremony. I told them I wouldn't say the vows, so no one who didn't already know I was unwilling attended. They threw a reception for everyone else."

"You went?"

I nodded. "Got drunk and told anyone who would listen that I didn't want to get married, but they either thought I was joking, or wanted to believe I was joking. Same difference, really."

"Why?" he asked. "Why force you into a marriage you don't want?"

"Served two purposes. Punished me for refusing to accept Pietro, 'rewarded' Paul for some job well done, I guess. He was obsessed with possessing me, didn't care that I wasn't into it. They all figured I would cave eventually. Obviously they underestimated the depths of my stubbornness."

Liam nods, accepting the explanation. "Well, that sucks."

"Agreed."

"Didn't your mom know you didn't want to marry him?"

I nod once, lips pressed firmly together. "Yep, she sure did."

He shakes his head. "That's fucked up. I'm sorry."

"Life sucks and then you die, right?" I take another sip of beer, then decide, fuck it, and finally take a bite of my sandwich.

"I'm sorry," he says again, and I frown at him, confused.

"You said that already."

"No, not for that. I mean… the tree thing," he specifies. "I didn't realize at the time, obviously, about Paul—"

Now it's my turn to stop him. "Oh, no, don't. Don't do that. I'm not some delicate flower, I'm honestly used to Paul, and I don't... I don't want you to treat me like…."

I'm not exactly sure how to finish—a battered woman? A victim? I don't want to use any of those words to describe myself, but he doesn't make me, as he nods, understanding my meaning.

Just to clarify, he adds, "I'm not like Paul."

I meet his gaze and hold it. "I didn't think you were."

Missing a beat, he admits, "I did like pinning you to that tree though."

I snort, like the delicate fucking flower I am. "I liked being pinned against that tree."

"I like that you give as good as you get," he tells me.

"Paul does not."

Something flits across his face but I don't have time to process it before he's stoic again. "Paul is shit and not really your husband. We don't have to talk about Paul anymore."

I nod. I don't like talking about Paul, either. "What about you?" I ask. "Girlfriend? Wife? Boyfriend?"

He smirks on that last part, and I'm glad, because it was slightly risky. "None of those," he tells me.

"That's good."

"Is it?" he asks, one golden brow shooting up.

"Well, any of those might object to the tree pinning," I point out.

"True enough," he allows.

I drink a little more beer.

"Sorry it's not wine," he puts in playfully.

I narrow my eyes at him as I set my beer back down on the table. "Did you take my chicken parm out of the oven?"

He nods, unapologetic. "I did. Didn't want you to die. I'd have to find a show or something to fill my evenings."

I bite back a smile. "What will you do now that I don't need your protection anymore?"

He shrugs, slowly bringing his beer to his mouth for a sip, never breaking eye contact.

I'm not sure what we're doing here, exactly, and a wave of nerves threatens to hit. I don't want to be nervous, so I dodge it by, well, diving right in.

"Planning on stalking me tonight?"

He's not at all sorry for the stalking. I'm not surprised. "Unless something better comes up."

I smile, slow and suggestive. I'm pretty sure I'm already in too deep, but I'm not about to admit that or back down now. I'll figure it out as I go. "What constitutes better?"

He flicks a glance at the food on the table in front of us. "Not sandwiches."

I smile again, looking at my own turkey sandwich. Turkey. Cold turkey. Cold feet.

I don't have cold feet, but I also don't have my own bed.

"There is the small matter that I don't actually have a house," I point out.

He seems unconcerned. "We don't need a house. We'll cross that bridge when we get to it."

I picture him taking me against the tree in a loincloth, his hair loose, my fingers digging into his shoulders.

As I'm amusing myself with mental images of him pulling a kinky Tarzan, he says, "Tell me something else about you."

"Like what?"

"How old were you when this shit happened?"

"The marriage shit?" He nods. "I was 18."

Liam scowls. "Jesus."

I try to keep it light. "You mean you weren't married at 18?"

It's like he tries to respond to my lightness, but isn't quite making it. "Weird, I realize. Why do you hate Pietro?"

I don't want to talk about Pietro and I don't want to get heavy. I want smoldering eye contact and kinky tree sex.

"Because I'm an excellent judge of character," I deadpan, hoping he'll drop it.

Liam appears completely unmoved by my wit, and he's also waiting for a better answer.

I sigh heavily, but figure I might as well get it out of the way. "He's... he's pure evil. He was friends with my dad back then. He was a Judas, but my dad trusted him. He has an appetite for power above all else and no loyalty. He's a snake."

"He betrayed your father?"

I nod. "Helped the guys who set him up. Led him right to them, knowing what they were going to do. If Pietro wouldn't have helped them, my father would still be alive."

"Your mom, she knew?"

"She denies it, but she knew. She had already locked onto him since he was rising to power, so she couldn't very well *admit* it without seeming like the faithless sellout she is."

"You obviously did not."

"Obviously. Look how well that turned out for me." I smile derisively. "But I'm alive. I do enough heinous shit to get by."

"We do what we have to," he reasons.

I glance up at him, wondering what his story is. "You do what you have to?"

He nods without a word, watching me. The moment stretches on longer than I expect it to, then his gaze drops to the untouched sandwich in front of him and I *feel* him withdraw, like it's a physical act. Even though I feel the shift, I'm still surprised when he suddenly says, "I have to go."

I rear back in surprise, my jaw dropping open a couple inches. "What? Now?"

The chair scrapes against the floor and he stands, nodding.

I'm so confused, I don't even move. I don't stand. I don't know what I did, what I said. My mouth opens to ask, but nothing comes out.

In the center of the table is a black wire basket with suggestion cards and pencils. He grabs one of each and jots something down. "If he comes back, if he tries anything and I'm not there to see it, call this number."

"It's yours?" I look at the card when he hands it to me, but I'm still reeling.

He nods. "Don't come back to the junkyard. I can't be seen with you there, you'll get us both in deep shit."

I want to ask what happened, or at least whether or not I'll see him again. Right now it doesn't feel like I will, and I'm so confused, because I'm sure he was planning on leaving with me just minutes ago.

I finally start to stand, but he just gives me one last, almost remorseful parting look, and makes his way to the door.

CHAPTER SEVEN
Liam

I'm grumpy as hell as I head into Raj's office, but I doubt I look any surlier than I usually do as I stop and stand at attention in front of his desk.

"You wanted to see me," I state.

"Yes." He's distracted, fingering papers in a stack as he quickly scans the tops. Finally he stops and looks up at me. "You can sit."

I prefer to stand, so I don't.

After a couple seconds, he looks up at me, then shrugs. One of the things I like about Raj is that he isn't a tiny man with a power struggle 'cause he thinks he's got something to prove. I can't stomach working for that type.

"Lance says you had a visitor."

Goddamn motherfucking Lance.

"I took care of it," I say simply, hoping that's enough and we don't have to get into it.

He murmurs something decidedly unconvinced. "I believe I told you not to hurt her."

All this mess with Paul makes me a touch more defensive

about that, but I can't afford to show it. "I didn't."

"Lance says differently."

"Why don't you tell me what Lance said then," I say evenly, not liking this little guessing game.

Raj looks at me disapprovingly, removing his glasses and setting them on top of his stack of papers. "That you…" He pauses, unsure how to word it, maybe hoping I'll save him from having to, but I don't. "—slept with her. Which seems… improbable given your specific directions not to be *seen*."

"I wasn't." I'm not sure how much of the truth to tell. Truth is, I can't figure out what Raj is thinking when it comes to Annabelle. Seems like he used to be close to her, but now he can't accept her innocence in her stepfather's world.

Raj quirks a dark eyebrow. "Then perhaps I've been doing sex all wrong."

Expressionless, I make a snap decision and go with it. "I went back after that night. The following night after work. Just to make sure I was right about what I'd reported back. I didn't sleep with her; I saw her husband hurting her. I stepped in. It was easier to tell Lance I slept with her."

"You spoke with her?"

"Briefly. She isn't working for Pietro. She hates him. Blames him for her father's death. Not to mention he made her marry an abusive prick. I can't say she'd be much use, given that she doesn't seem to have much contact with him, but… if given the chance, she'd switch sides."

He's eyeing me up but he doesn't unsettle me. "We don't need anyone on his side."

I shrug. "I don't know the girl, but you seem to have a history. Just thought you might be interested in another way."

Raj shakes his head and sighs, looking at his desktop. "My

history is with a naïve young girl who doesn't exist anymore. Her husband is abusive, you say?"

I nod once, feeling a tick in my jaw and hoping he doesn't notice it.

"That's unfortunate," he says, looking worn.

"Her whole life seems to be," I state.

"What would we do with her?"

I shrug, like it doesn't mean much to me, but I'm excited that he's taking the bait. "Extra assurance? She knows the place inside and out, knows the people—she could help everything go smoothly, night of."

Raj considers it for several seconds, then shakes his head. "I don't believe she would go along with it. She's not cold enough. She would end up betraying us."

I don't know if she would, and I can't vouch for it. Then if something goes wrong, it's my neck on the line. Not to mention, if I cared enough to put my own neck on the line already, Raj wouldn't believe I'd let it go as easily as I will. Raj doesn't know me, and usually that's fine, but I don't want to suddenly make him skittish, make him start second guessing me. Not over some girl I barely know.

"All right," I say, easily enough. "It was just an idea. I thought you might have some sentimental attachment. Anyway, I've already taken care of it. She just wanted to thank me for stepping in with Paul. She won't be back around."

"She didn't question why you were following her in the first place?"

I pause, because I'm not sure how to answer this. "She thinks I *want* to fuck her."

"Do you?"

I shrug. "She's attractive. So are many others. Would I fuck her? Yes. Do I need to?" I snort, instead of answering.

This is easy for him to accept.

"She didn't seem to suspect anything?"

"She doesn't seem to give a single shit what we're doing here."

He frowns in thought. "Could be an act."

"It isn't."

His eyebrows rise, and he's skeptical of how confidently I answered. He isn't sure he can trust me right now. Maybe I've been compromised; maybe I'm as much a fucking schmuck as any other guy in the world, bewitched by a beautiful woman. What if I sell him out in the name of love and ruin everything?

I want to roll my eyes. Instead I smile, answering his unasked question. "I'm good at reading people."

The coldness in my eyes despite the smile maybe hints that I can read him, as well, because then he flushes and retrieves his glasses, suddenly busy with his papers again. "Yes, well. If she comes around again, I don't want to hear it from Lance."

"Got it. I should've said something myself, honestly it just didn't occur to me. Her visit wasn't about any of this."

He nods and is quiet long enough for me to understand I've been dismissed, so I turn to leave. Just as my hand touches the doorknob, Raj speaks again. "I can still count on you to show up that night, right?"

A cocktail of uncomfortable feelings trickle through me, but I barely spare him a glance over my shoulder as I open the door to leave.

"Of course."

Instead of camping outside Annabelle's house after work, I get food and go home.

As I devour my takeout, I try not to think about her plight. About *my* plight. I shouldn't even have a plight. This girl is a stranger to me—okay, not as much a stranger now as she had been before, but still not worth tanking my life over. She couldn't be. It wasn't an option.

I should have never gotten involved. I should've followed orders and followed her home the first night, and that should've been it. It wasn't my job to protect her. Now, because I got involved like a fucking rookie idiot, I have a moral fucking dilemma on my hands. Moral dilemmas aren't really my thing. I try to tell myself it isn't even *my* dilemma, because there's nothing I can actually *do* about anything. I may be a player in the game, but this is *not* my game.

It doesn't make me feel any better.

I do what I can to keep my mind off it—work out, shower, watch some television, but I can't shake thoughts of this damn girl and her plump, soft-looking goddamn lips. I can't shake visions of tiny little Paul trying to hurt and intimidate her. Images of her goading the man she despises, unafraid. That scares me more than it should. It doesn't when I'm outside in case she needs anything, but from this distance it scares me.

Eventually I decide, just to set my mind at ease, to drive by. He probably isn't even home. If I see that she's fine, I can stop thinking about it.

That's what I tell myself.

That's how I end up driving by her house, even after I told

myself I wouldn't anymore. That's how I end up parking my car up the road and creeping into her back yard to peek in her bedroom window, where the light's on. That's how I get stuck with the mental image of her curled up on her bed alone, reading a book and periodically glancing hopefully at the windows like she's watching for me.

Goddammit.

I should've kissed her at the deli. Could've done more than kiss her, I remind myself. Maybe I should've, just to get her out of my system. But it wouldn't have been right.

I scoff at myself. *Right.* Talk about a concept I haven't worried myself over for a long-ass time.

Can't twist yourself up over right and wrong in this line of work. They hire you for a job, you do the job, you move along. You keep your morality and your heart—if you have the misfortune of possessing one—out of it. If you can't, maybe you should find a new line of work.

I've never had a problem with it. Some guys struggle with it at some point, either way early, or way late in the game. Even a guy like Lance may crack eventually, have a crisis of conscience. Not me. This isn't even a crisis of conscience, that's the aggravating part. It's a goddamn crisis of libido.

That's what I tell myself.

She took me off guard by that goddamn tree, her and her weird-ass coping mechanisms. She laughs when Paul wants to kill her and flirts when an armed stranger has her pinned to a tree.

I wonder what it would take to make her show her fear. To break through her defenses.

I wonder if she'll be afraid when her world comes crashing down around her, and I'm standing at the gateway, not allowing her to escape the wreckage.

I wonder if she'll be afraid when she realizes I'm going to kill her.

CHAPTER EIGHT
Annabelle

I'm smack dab in the middle of a tense standoff when stupid Paul comes skulking into the bedroom.

I narrow my eyes at him over the edge of my book, but I don't speak. My eyes drop back to the page and I reread the last line. I want to finish the chapter, but now I can't focus because Paul is home and I'm not sure what he's going to do.

I haven't even seen him since the night Liam saved me. Beaten, soggy and humiliated, Paul had run away with his tail between his legs, and that's exactly where I wanted him to stay — away.

My eyes move across the page without absorbing a single word. Why is he here? Is he staying? What's his mood like? A dozen similar questions run across my mind, but I keep my eyes on my book so he doesn't try to talk to me either way.

I hear Paul drop his jeans and toss them into the laundry corner (there's a basket along the same wall, but he'd die before dropping his clothes into it). I sigh irritably, turning the page just for something to do.

"Gettin' good?"

I glance at him over the edge of the book again with dead eyes.

He attempts a half smile that comes across more as a grimace. "Your book. You always... start making noises when it gets good or starts aggravating you."

I stare.

"Little impatient noises," he adds, and I can't imagine why he's still talking. "It's cute."

Now I scowl, but I just go back to my book without replying. He's confusing me and that's probably what the bastard is going for, so I'll just ignore him.

Try to get me to lower my guard, motherfucker. Tell me I'm cute. Stupid cow.

"You know you were reading a book the first time I saw you?"

I can't believe he's still talking to me, and still nicely, when I'm only giving back unceasing disinterest. Also, I couldn't care less what I was doing when he first saw me. I wish I would've been ass-naked, fucking someone else, because then he probably wouldn't have fixated on owning me.

"You didn't see me," he continues, for some reason. "But you were so wrapped up in your book, and you kept sighing and glaring at the pages, and then a minute later you'd grin, all giddy, and you'd laugh, and you swore at it a time or two. I couldn't look away. I remember thinking that I'd bet you were that passionate in everything you did."

I'm not glaring anymore, but I'm not pretending to read anymore, either. I glance up at him uncertainly, not understanding this game.

Finally, Paul drops my gaze and says, "I brought food."

It's after ten, but I don't say that. Usually I would, but he seems like he's in a sad mood tonight, and I'm not in the mood to kick him.

I reluctantly put my book down on the bedside table and wrap my crocheted shawl around me, trekking behind him toward the door.

I steal one last glance back at the bedroom windows, but it's as fruitless as it has been all the other times I've looked tonight; Liam isn't there.

I wish I understood why.

Paul is unpacking containers on the kitchen counter and I catch a strong whiff of my favorite Italian takeout. We never get it because it's pricey and fattening and takes more than five minutes to pick and purchase.

Curious, I peek into the bag and see he even got a chocolate cannoli for dessert. Just one to split, because they're so sweet—a whole one gives me a tummy ache.

I finally speak, because my curiosity has gotten the best of me. "What's all this?"

"We haven't had it in a while." He scoots my container of fettuccine closer to me. "It used to be your favorite."

I'm puzzled by this sudden trip down memory lane, and even more baffled by his desire to drag me along, when I was never along for the ride to begin with. There were no good memories of us, I'd made sure of it. I was venom in a white lace dress at our sham wedding, and I never got nicer. If he retained even a hand full of nice memories, he must have collected them through pure delusion.

Years of carefully nurtured hatred and disdain, and here he was, reminiscing.

Without waiting for him, I take my food over to the table

and sit down. I forgot to grab a drink, and a moment later he emerges from the fridge with two sodas instead of just one for himself. He pushes one across the table at me, reminding me of when he used to do that all the time.

I'd forgotten about that.

My distrust of him grows by the second. Fear suddenly slices through me and I'm caught off guard by the thought, *Is this it? Is this the night he finally kills me?*

My favorite meal for a last meal, reminiscing over nice—if one-sided—memories like we're already at my funeral. Serving me a drink like he used to when he didn't hate me so much.

I didn't know how he was going to react to what Liam did. He was accustomed to me coming up against him, but I'm small, I can't hurt him. Liam stepping in, that was something different. That wasn't even "pick on someone your own size," that was David and Goliath.

What if it was too much?

What if I'd finally pushed him too far—and not even through my own actions?

This wasn't how I expected it. Not calm. Not premeditated. It had to be impulsive, in anger. He didn't deserve to take me out anyway, but this cool, premeditated bullshit—fuck that.

"Marlene busy tonight?"

He doesn't tense at the blow, he sags. Sighs. Drops his fork. No anger. I haven't riled him. He looks sad. Maybe she dumped him.

He doesn't say anything so I just keep eating.

After watching me take four bites, unconcerned with whether he eats or not, there's finally an edge of sarcasm when he asks, "How's Thor?"

I can't help smiling, and to be honest, I don't try. I smile, big and unapologetic, and take another bite.

He doesn't need to know Thor no longer comes around.

Paul sulks. Pushes his pasta around with a sour look on his face. "How'd you even meet that guy anyway?"

"Oh, you know, at the deli counter, buying cold cuts."

He is unimpressed. "Fine. Guess it's none of my business. I'm just your husband."

"I don't ask how you meet yours, you don't ask how I meet mine."

This seems to jar him, like he's never *once* considered he's not the only one who fucks around. "How… How many others have there been?"

"Does it matter?"

He looks so disenchanted I almost feel bad for him.

Well, no, not really, but it is amusing.

He's trying to wrap his mind around what I've just said, head shaking in denial. "This is not what I wanted."

"Same." I'm glib, coldly meeting his gaze.

His head drops into his hands. I roll my eyes at his dramatics and go to the fridge for more parmesan to shake over my pasta.

While Paul processes whatever emotions he's dealing with over there, I enjoy my pasta. It's good. Maybe not as good as I remember, but it feels like my world is different now, bleaker, and even delicious pasta doesn't hold the same appeal.

It's disappointing.

I almost wish he hadn't bought it, then I could always imagine it *would've* been as good as I remember.

A dark, dismal cloud settles over my head all of a sudden. It drapes itself around my shoulders like a physical weight, and suddenly I'm exhausted.

THE LAST BOSS' DAUGHTER

There's still nearly half a plate of pasta but I don't want it. Shoving it to the center of the table, I announce, "I'm going to bed."

"Wait." The sound of chair dragging across the floor makes me tense. I don't stop, I keep going to the bedroom, but he follows me.

I run through the phone number Liam left me. I kept the paper it was written on, but I also memorized it, just to be safe.

"I'm tired," I say, wanting to be left alone.

He grabs my arm—habit—but lets go as soon as I glare at him over my shoulder. We've made it to the bedroom. He raises his hands as if in surrender, implying he meant no harm.

"What?" I snap, tired of the guesswork.

He sighs and sort of glances around, as if for someone to help him talk to me. Obviously there is no one, and his gaze wanders back to me, but he looks a little lost, a little helpless.

"This isn't…. I don't want things to be like this."

I don't dignify that with a response.

He continues. "What if we… what if we went on, like, a date night or something?"

I'm grossed out that he used the words "date night," but much more so that he used them in reference to something *we* would do, like an actual fucking married couple.

Instead of showing the disgust I'm swimming in, I display the complete and utter fucking befuddlement with a blank stare. "Why?"

It ruffles him, like it was meant to. Finally something familiar happens and he clams up, growing angrily defensive, like a little boy who answered wrong in class and got laughed at. "I don't know. Jesus Christ, I try to suggest something nice…"

"We don't do nice things, Paul."

"And it's so wrong to want to change that?" His voice rises now. I'm surprised it's taken this long. He usually resorts to yelling much faster. "You're my—" He stops short of calling me his wife, and I watch him wrestle with his temper for a minute.

This is new. He usually lets it run wild and free, but I guess the fear of Liam provides better incentive than I expected.

Once he's had a minute to reign it in, he continues more evenly. "I have a proposition. Something for you to think about."

I'm silent, but I'm listening.

"What if we gave this a real try? You stop fucking Thor, I'll stop fucking Marlene, and we could maybe give this a real go. See what happens."

I'm completely shocked. I don't show it. I remain impassive, unsure how to play this. I couldn't be less interested—if he stopped sleeping with that girl, he'd want to sleep with me, and ew. I also have no interest whatsoever in growing a relationship with him. He's the worst. We've never been anything. I wasn't interested at the beginning, anywhere in the middle, and I'm damn sure not interested at the end.

I don't know how to say that. I want to laugh, but he seems as sincere as I've seen Paul, so I don't. Who knows, maybe Marlene is sweet enough not to engage his Hulk side. Maybe we bring out the worst in each other. He certainly brings out the worst in me. This can't be his best side, or no one would ever want him, and women have. For some reason.

Gross.

The kindest thing I can do is turn and walk away from him, so that's what I do. I drop my shawl over by my bedside table and climb into bed, digging under my fortress of blankets. I'm too tired for him to spring shit like this on me.

He stands in the doorway for a long time. Or, it feels like a long time. Maybe it's only a few minutes, but they're long, awkward minutes. Finally he gives up and heads back to the kitchen.

I close my eyes and search for my safety. It's here somewhere. My eyes open and I check the windows one last time.

Disappointed, I close my eyes and steady my breathing.

My eyes open again, parted by some instinct, and I'm not sure, but I saw a flash of something at the edge of the window.

I keep my eyes open that time, staring at the spot. Nothing moves, but I'm sure I saw something, so I throw back my covers and pad over to the window. Pressing close to the pane of glass, I look, but see nothing. A woman on a mission, I unlock the window and lift it, popping my head outside to check both directions.

Nothing.

Maybe it had just been wishful thinking. Maybe I saw what I wanted to see.

I frown, disappointed, and head back to bed.

CHAPTER NINE
Annabelle

Another week passes and nothing happens.

No Liam sightings, no sudden, inexplicable love for Paul. After a couple of days without interest, Paul went back to Marlene.

Maybe that's why he did this. Maybe he was so mad at me for not jumping at the offer to suddenly try for a relationship I had never wanted, he decided to punish me. He couldn't inflict bodily harm on me, since he still thinks I'm having an affair with Liam, but he *could* drag me to my old home and force me to sit through a 'family dinner' with the snakes who currently reside in it.

Pietro was already here when we got here, and—to my horror—approached us as soon as we walked in the door.

He didn't acknowledge me though. Didn't even look at me. It was like Paul walked in alone. Pietro came over, put an arm around his shoulder to pull him in real close, and hauled him away. I caught, "Now tell me how this happened," before Paul laughed a little nervously and they disappeared inside my dad's old study.

Now I'm sitting on an ugly fucking floral couch that my mom picked to replace our old one. She remodeled everything after my father's death, systematically, room by room. First she just wanted to replace the carpets, then the downstairs bathroom, then the upstairs bathrooms really needed revamping as well. The entryway, so outdated! And before long, the only thing left of my father's home was the crystal chandelier hanging in the foyer.

I haven't been in this house for dinner in a long time. When Paul and I first got thrown together, we came over biweekly, I think just so everyone could make sure I hadn't run away. I was so furious at every single one of them for not stopping the wedding that I wouldn't speak, wouldn't eat. I sat there glaring at anyone who would look at me, and smacking Paul's hand away when he inexplicably tried to caress it on the table. Maybe he thought I wouldn't do that in front of my family. Maybe he thought I'd be meeker.

Eventually he gave up on that lost cause and we stopped coming to the horrible dinners.

Then we only came over for holidays. Not how I wanted to spend my holidays anyway, but it didn't matter. There was no better alternative.

For our first Christmas together, my mother had given me the gown I was christened in. I held the soft fabric in my hands and stared at it, horrified at the prospect of birthing a half-Paul child to stuff into it. As soon as my doctor's office opened after its Christmas break, I made an appointment to go on the pill.

Shaking off the memories being in this place stirs in me, I stand. I'm bored and I don't know where my mother is. Paul is still closed up in the study with Pietro.

I make my way back to the foyer and gaze up at the massive chandelier. On Christmas Eve, we always put Santa's milk and cookies on a little round table underneath it. Normally Mom had a doily and a vase of fresh flowers on the table, but for Christmas Eve we used it for Santa. Sometimes I left him a little thank you note, in anticipation of the presents he would give me.

Even the damn table is gone, replaced by one of metal and glass. A new vase full of flowers rests on top.

My heart accelerates as I make my way upstairs. I never go upstairs. The halls I used to make my father chase me down are up there, and my shrieks of laughter as he lumbered after me still echo off the walls. My childhood bedroom is up there, though I'm sure it's been remodeled into something unrecognizable at this point. She probably gave it to her new daughter; not because there were no other bedrooms, but because it had been mine.

Sorrow washes over me the moment I step foot on the landing upstairs. I consider turning back; the last thing I need is more sadness.

But I go forward. I can see the heavy oak door of my old bedroom. More memories, insignificant shit: painting my nails at the desk in the corner, listening to pop music and gazing lovingly at the photo of the boy I had a crush on, curling up in my bed after an inconsequential fight with my mom.

The world had been alive and full of possibilities for the girl who lived here. She could've never ended up like me, and yet, here we are.

I push open the door. The creak as it swings open sounds amplified and I look around the hall, paranoid that someone will come, like I'm doing something I shouldn't be. Trespassing.

I feel like I am.

This isn't mine anymore. I don't belong here.

I step inside anyway, and surprise floods me at the sight of the same delicate pink walls, the same posters and picture frames

I had decorated with.

Nothing has changed.

My room is untouched.

The girl who slept here no longer exists, but somehow, all of her belongings remain unmolested.

I hate myself for the faint trickle of tenderness that pools around my heart. *Why*? Why would she leave this room, of all the rooms, as is? She can't even have an *accent table* that reminds her of our family, but she left my whole bedroom exactly as I'd left it.

And I do mean exactly.

Stretched across the unmade bed is the nightgown I wore the night before my goddamn wedding. If I picked it up and brought it to my face, it would probably still smell faintly of the optimistic hopes and dreams of a girl who was certain her mother could never go through with betraying her so horrendously.

I step away from the bed and hasten over to my dresser. If everything is still the same, that means…

A smile transforms my face as I pull out the diamond and ruby ring Daddy gave me for my 16th birthday. It was the last gift I ever got from him, and I'd regretted not wearing it the day of the wedding so I'd still have it. Afterwards, I was too angry to go back for my things. The following day when I was supposed to go pack, I'd been too traumatized. I hadn't left the bed. Three days later, I still hadn't. Eventually they gave up and Paul brought home a suitcase full of things my mother had picked out from my dresser. That was it, every belonging I brought with me from my old life into my new one. I'd never stepped foot in my old bedroom for anything again in the ten years between then and now.

The ring still glistens as I move my hand in the light. I don't wear Paul's wedding ring, so I put it on my bare ring finger. It's as beautiful as I remember.

"What are you doing in here?"

I start, clasping my hand protectively as I turn to see Sofia, my 7-year-old half sister. She has a touch of my mom in her, but it's Pietro's chilly eyes that look out at me.

"This used to be my room," I say, since I really don't have an explanation for what I'm doing in here.

She glances around at an old room that means nothing to her. "Yeah, Mom told me. We always keep this door closed."

Since she seems to want me out, I leave. She follows, closing the door behind us. I imagine in some cases she would want to show me, her older sister, what *her* bedroom looks like, since I've never seen it and we're already up here. She expresses no such desire, and we make our way downstairs without another word.

My discomfort only grows from here. I follow her to the kitchen where my mom has already started on the wine. I wonder why she didn't share. Wine would probably make me more pleasant company, even though she's drinking red and I strongly prefer white.

When I come in, instead of offering me any, she plugs the wine and puts it away.

"To chill," she says. "We'll have some with dinner."

"Is that ever happening?" I ask.

Pietro, Paul, and whomever else they have locked away in there haven't emerged.

Taking a leaf from my book, she ignores me and flits away to pretend to do something at the other end of the counter.

Then, reconsidering, she turns back. "Please be pleasant tonight. Pietro has had a bad week and the last thing this family needs is you making things worse."

I'm suddenly glad she *didn't* give me wine, because the glass would shatter in my hand right now and a perfectly good serving would be all over the ceramic Tuscan tile.

If looks could kill, my mother would join her first husband right now.

I turn and quit the room.

I'm angry. So angry. *Furious*. My face is hot with it and there's a strangled cry of fury trapped in my throat.

I hate her.

I hate all of them.

Just as I'm fixing to storm outside and, I don't know, *run* home, the study door opens.

I catch a glimpse inside. The once red walls are blue now. The door closes and Pietro is looking at me.

It always feels like a stare-down when I don't adequately avoid his gaze. Once we've made eye contact, I won't look away, no matter how much I want to. Won't let him think there's any part of me that submits to him.

"Annabelle," he says, pleasantly enough.

I don't return the greeting. My jaw locks, my teeth smashing together. In the jumble of frantic heartbeats I notice my breathing is getting irregular. I try to bring it down a notch, since this is how my panic attacks start. It's been probably a year since I've had one, but all the ingredients for one are certainly here tonight.

My stomach feels tight. Sick. I won't have an attack in front of him. He'll see it as weakness, and as far as he's concerned, I'm motherfucking Sparta.

In my mind, at least.

I don't really care what I look like in his.

But then the bastard takes a step toward me and drapes an arm across my shoulder like he did Paul's earlier. I'm too stunned to react and somehow I'm being led down the hall along with him.

"I hear you've been a bad girl."

He says it lightly enough, but I don't trust it. My mind blanks before racing through all the things I've done lately that he could object to. I don't know how to respond because I'm not sure what he's referring to.

"You're gonna have to be more specific," I shoot back, as if unruffled.

He laughs, and the sound makes my skin crawl. His arm still draped around me probably helps.

After a moment, when I don't offer anymore or respond, he says, "Good wives don't cuckold their husbands."

I smile. "And what do *you* know about good wives?"

This slight to my mother should offend him, anger him, but his grin only stretches wider. He looks bizarrely pleased with my response, and for a split second, my confidence drops.

"You don't like me much, do you?" he asks.

The sheer idiocy of this question strikes me momentarily speechless.

Only a moment though, then I reply, "I'm not much for the company of killers."

I haven't even annoyed him. His brown eyes are cold while mine must be alight with barely contained loathing.

"Funny, that's not what I heard," he answers evenly.

I remain unimpressed, but I'm not sure how to take that. I have the uncomfortable feeling he knows something I don't, and the last thing I want is for him to know that.

"Come on," he says, almost brightly. "Let's eat."

CHAPTER TEN
Liam

It's been a week since they started tailing her.

I haven't been able to get near her. Haven't been able to reach out at all. I'm sure she has no idea, but red flags are going up around every lobe in my brain. Are they watching her, or watching for me?

After a week, I've pegged the weak link. Two of the guys they have on her are pretty good, but the third fucks around on his phone a lot. He gets the night shift, so it's boring for him anyway, but if I'm going in, that's when.

I shouldn't try. It's reckless and dangerous and frankly stupid.

At the end of the day, my belief that I'm better than them, and some concern for her that I don't want to deal with, drive me to do the stupid thing. I do it as smartly as I can, parking on the street behind her house and cutting through a neighbor's yard. I'm thankful they don't have a motion light and it goes smoothly, but I don't know how I'm going to get in quietly. The kid watching her is out front, and she just turned on the bathroom light a couple of minutes ago. I can't get in the bathroom.

Window's too high and on the side of the house. I can't go in either door, because they're on the front and side of the house—again, kid'll see me. I can't bust out a window, because that's not subtle and they may hear me.

I also don't know if they have the house bugged. I'm not going to take the time to search it; I'm just going to assume the answer is yes and be doubly safe.

I want to kiss the fuck out of her when I get to the back window and find it unlocked. It's not hard to pop out the screen without a lot of noise, and a minute later I'm inside.

The shower's running. I stifle a groan at the prospect of finding her naked. I don't want to find her naked, ready to step into the shower. That's fucking mean.

This is so much easier than I imagined it being. I make it to the bathroom door and turn the knob, opening it as quietly as I can.

Her back is to me and she is, in fact, naked except for her panties and about to step into the steamy shower.

I don't want to scare her, but more than that, I don't want to alert the guy watching her that anything is happening. So just as she goes to shimmy out of her panties, I lunge forward and grab her, clapping a hand over her mouth and pulling her back against the hard plane of my body.

She struggles and tries to scream, but before she can I'm whispering in her ear. "It's me."

She stills. Her chest works hard, and I'm sort of crushing her right breast with my arm.

I give her a minute to calm down. I feel her relax against me, her left hand coming to rest on the arm gripping her hard across the chest. She doesn't know why I'm here, sneaking into her house and grabbing her, but she doesn't question it. Doesn't worry that

THE LAST BOSS' DAUGHTER

I'd ever be here to hurt her.

My hand still covers her mouth but I let go of the grip I have on her. I let her turn around, backed up against the wall in the small space, and she doesn't even try to cover herself.

I resist the urge to look and use my free hand to bring a finger to my lips, warning her to be quiet.

Her eyes grow wider but she nods, and I move my hand away from her mouth. She's silent, waiting for my direction. It sort of kills me how much she trusts me.

As if to hint how much she shouldn't trust me, my gaze finally drops. Now that I know she'll be quiet, I can look at her.

Time slows down for us, because I'm a fucking idiot.

She takes a breath when my gaze hits her tits, and before I can think better of it, my hands are drawn to them, covering them, thumbing the pebbled nipples. A breath rushes out of her and she closes her eyes, resting her head back against the wall.

I measure the weight of them in my hands, caressing her flesh. I move in closer, pressing against her mostly bare body. I release her tits, bringing my arms up on either side of her, trapping her against the wall.

I want to kiss her so goddamn bad. She arches against me, craving the same contact.

This is not what I came for.

Before things can get too far out of hand, I take a step back. She covers herself, as if chilled, and I reach back to retrieve the bra and t-shirt she left abandoned on the edge of the sink.

She dresses quickly and reaches to turn off the shower but I grab her, stopping her with a shake of my head.

She's frowning now, really confused, but she obeys and follows me. I hold up a hand for her to stay in the hall. I want to check out the living room window, just to make sure the kid hasn't noticed anything. His face is illuminated by the glow of his phone; he hasn't moved.

I go back to get Annabelle in the hall, and I don't know exactly what I'm doing, because I can't just break her out. Any longer than it would take for her to shower and even the dipshit outside might start to wonder what's going on. If I kill him, her whole goddamn family will come after me. I don't need that headache.

I climb out the window first so I can help her out. She doesn't know what's going on but follows me without reservation. I could be leading her to her death, and she'd follow me there like a fucking puppy.

I shouldn't have saved her. Now she thinks I'm her hero when I'm anything but.

I haul her out back but it's not far enough. There's a thicket of woods in the yard of a neighboring house on that back street where I parked. I consider just taking her to my car, but I strike the idea down and head for the wooded area instead.

She's slower than I am, so I grab her hand to pull her along.

And then here we are, back amongst the trees. That first meeting, pinning her against the tree comes to mind, and I want to do it again, but I push down my baser urges.

Quietly, unsure, she asks, "What's going on?"

"You're being watched."

Her eyebrows rise, since, well, I've been watching her.

"Not by me. Not our guys. Pietro's."

Now she scowls. "Why?"

"That's what I want to know," I tell her. I watch her, too. It's not that I don't trust her, 'cause I more or less do or I wouldn't be putting my neck on the line for her, but… you can never be too careful. I'm not as trusting as she is.

She shakes her head, gazing off at nothing, trying to think. "I don't know. I think Paul told him I'm having an affair. Maybe they're watching for the guy—well, you. In which case, you *really* should not be sneaking in my bedroom window. I'm not going to leave it open anymore."

"There's no other reason you can think of?" I demand.

Shrugging helplessly, she says, "What other reason could there be?"

I sigh, looking at a spot beyond her head. "I'm not going to be able to come around with them watching the house. What if Paul set this up on purpose? Has he been acting strangely?"

"He's Paul, he always acts strangely." She pauses, frowns. "I mean... I guess he has been extra strange lately. You think, what, he has guys watching the place so you can't protect me?"

I don't know, and she knows I don't know, but I watch the implications of that sink in on her face and I want to hit someone. A line of someones. As many people as there are standing between Annabelle and me protecting her.

Goddammit.

I don't know if I'm more enraged by the possibility of Paul or Pietro keeping me out so she's at Paul's mercy, or the steely fucking resolve I have not to let that happen. Both are extremely problematic.

"Fuck," she says softly.

I nod, because I was thinking the same thing.

She looks at the road. "I could run."

"You won't make it. You don't have the resources and you'd have maybe an hour before every guy on Pietro's payroll, cops included, are hunting you down."

"Well, fuck. What the hell do I do?"

It's not much, but I reach into one of my pockets and pull

out the only safeguard I could provide her. "This isn't sufficient," I tell her as I hand her the stun gun. She looks at it as it transfers into her hand, then back at me. "If he attacks you, you can use this. It's a big if though. You're not going to be able to carry it around out in the open, or he'll obviously know. Even if you can use it, he's not going to be incapacitated long enough for me to get to you unless I'm right around the corner."

Dread fills her features and she looks at the small measure of defense again.

"If you have to use it, call me immediately. They might have your house bugged, so just say… lightning bug," I say, somehow the first thing to cross my mind. "I'll come as fast as I can."

"I don't like this."

She doesn't feel safe. *I* can't keep her safe. That fucking infuriates me.

"I'm going to come up with something better," I tell her. "This is just until then."

I don't expect her to get vulnerable. I don't know why. But when she fists my shirt in her hands and burrows into me for comfort, something expands and explodes inside my chest. She tilts her head back, looking fucking beautiful and vulnerable and open, and she says, "I don't wanna go back there."

I hate everything about the world, because she has to.

And I can't do a goddamn thing about it.

Angry at my powerlessness, plagued with a yearning I've never had to deal with before, I fist my hand in her hair and jerk it back, tilting her face up toward mine. A breath of surprise, but no protest, and she gazes up at me, inviting me with her eyes.

My free hand comes up and I brush my rough thumb across her soft, smooth cheek. I don't want to identify the rush of tenderness I'm experiencing, so I call it a new strain of lust. My thumb brushes across her plump lower lip, catching it. She doesn't break eye contact, but turns her head just enough to pull the tip of my thumb into her warm, wet mouth. Lust surges through me as her mouth closes around it, and I see what I'm feeling reflected back in her warm brown eyes.

    I let go of her hair and walk her up against the nearest tree. She never breaks eye contact as her back hits the rough bark, and I want to fuck her more than I want to stay sane, apparently. I'm still pretty sure I shouldn't, but I'm damn sure going to kiss her.

    I hold back for a few seconds, thinking of all the very good reasons I have for *not* kissing her, but none hold up when her fingers tentatively come to rest on my sides, tugging me toward her ever so lightly.

    She's waited long enough for this. Fuck, so have I.

    I dip my head toward hers and her lips part for me, soft and eager. She winds a hand around my neck, pulling herself up closer to my height and our lips brush, soft at first. Moaning against my lips, she pushes her tits against me, tempting the hell out of me. I catch one in my palm, kneading it as my tongue sweeps into her mouth. Things pick up, each of us a little more desperate with every breath.

    I want her, and I don't give a damn why that's a bad idea.

    My hands skim her sides, moving over the curve of her ass. I lift her, planting myself between her thighs and pinning her against the tree, like the first time, 'cept the first time I didn't have my tongue halfway down her throat, her fingers moving through my hair, listening to her little moans of pleasure.

    The hardness of my erection is obvious as I push between her legs. She groans, one hand dropping to grip me through the fabric.

    Hissing, I slam her against the tree. She cries out, quietly, and I open my eyes to make sure I didn't hurt her. Her eyes blaze with passion and her hand works the button on my pants.

"We can't," I manage.

"Yes, we can," she says, freeing the button and shoving her hand down my pants.

Jesus, that's hard to say no to.

"Annabelle..."

"Please," she murmurs, bending to kiss the curve of my neck as her soft hand strokes my length.

Jesus Christ.

I pull back, but it's the hardest goddamn thing I've ever done.

I let her down gently, trying to ignore her crestfallen expression as her bare feet touch the forest floor.

"Why?" she asks, and I feel like an asshole. She's turned on and flushed and I'm rejecting her.

I can't tell her.

It's selfish as hell, but I don't want her to stop looking at me the way she does.

Averting my gaze, not wanting to see the hurt expression, I say, "You've gotta get back. Before they notice anything..."

It's even meaner. I pull her out of a place of passion and pleasure, and remind her of the bullshit life she has to go back to.

She keeps her head down for a moment, and when she looks up again, her face is clear. Expressionless.

Guilt wallops me. I want to rewind the moment and keep going. I want to fuck her. Who cares if I feel guilty afterward? I should. It's not as if my betrayal will be any easier for her just because I stopped.

I don't want to be one more person who's betrayed her. I don't want to finish the job.

If I don't, someone else will. No matter how I feel, no matter what I want, I can't save her.

I don't let her see how twisted up I am. My face as blank as hers, I get in front of her and lead the way back to her yard. I try to help her inside, but she swats my goddamn hand away like I'm Paul.

I don't climb inside with her. It's like there's a pit of acid in my gut, seeping out and eating away at everything it touches.

And I was so goddamn distracted I didn't realize I couldn't speak to her once we made it back to her house, so I can't even say goodbye.

I don't even know if I'll see her again.

She closes the window and turns away without so much as another glance. I feel a sliver of what Paul must feel every day, and it burns in my gut. She stops beside the bed, with her back to me, and pulls the t-shirt over her head, dropping it into the floor. She unclasps the bra and lets it drop, then pushes her panties down.

I don't look away, and she turns around, giving me one last look at her, fully naked. She meets my gaze, still blank, and then turns and goes back to the shower.

It's stupid and reckless and pointless, since she hates me right now, but I try the window. If she didn't lock it, I'm going to climb in the goddamn window and get in that shower with her, and if the dipshit with the cell phone puts a bullet in my head while I'm fucking her, so be it.

It's locked.

Regret rocks me and I wait another minute before I turn and make my way back to my car.

CHAPTER ELEVEN
Annabelle

Paul doesn't kill me, which I guess is a good thing.

He comes home late that night, but I'm already in bed. The stun gun remains hidden in my bedside drawer, but I lack the energy to reach for it. Turns out I don't need to; he goes to sleep.

I wonder if there's any chance he doesn't know I'm being watched.

I close my eyes and try to sleep, but all I can see are flashes of Liam. I touch the breast his fingers squeezed hours earlier and look out the window. I know he isn't out there now. I don't even want him to be, not if Pietro's guys are watching the house, but no matter how good I usually am at guarding my feelings, I can't seem to ignore the burn of rejection. I don't understand it. I know he wanted me, I could feel the physical evidence. Literally held the hot, hard proof in the palm of my hand.

I sigh and go to roll over, but I remember Paul is there so I stay put. Looking at his gross face isn't going to make me feel any better. In fact, it only makes me think how amused he would be if he knew that my grand love affair was with a man who wouldn't even fuck me.

I finally drift off to sleep, but it's broken and full of bad dreams. Come morning I'm exhausted, and not at all prepared for my mother to call me and tell me today's the day we go dress shopping.

As much as I want to say no, I also feel like a prisoner in the former sanctuary of my own home. I don't know if they're listening or watching. It makes me paranoid, because I don't even know why it's happening.

"Perk up!" my mother says from the driver's seat, making me cringe.

"There's not enough coffee in the world."

A moment passes before she says, "You must've been up late last night."

"I went to bed early, actually."

"Have you thought about what kind of dress you'd like?"

"No." Dress shopping has been the last thing on my mind, what with never knowing if I'd see the light of another day and all.

I wonder if she knows. She obviously knows something, but how much? I can't envision Pietro confiding in her as he loosens his tie and unbuttons his sleeves after a long day of work, but maybe he does.

Does she know her husband has men watching my house? Does she know it might be my husband who wanted them there to assure no knight in shining armor comes to my rescue if he decides one night he's had enough of my shit? Does she know her husband may ultimately be responsible for my death, just like he was my father's?

"How's Paul?" she asks, like there's even a chance of me answering, let alone caring.

There isn't and I don't.

After a moment passes, she says, "Pietro says you two have been having problems."

I'm too tired for this shit.

"Paul and I have never had anything *but* problems," I state, resting my head against the window.

She's quiet for another few seconds, then she asks quietly, "Who's this other guy?"

My pulse quickens at the mere mention, however indirect, of Liam. I imagine another lifetime where we would've talked about a man I had feelings for, but this is not that lifetime.

I don't answer, but I'm tempted to. The problem with being as isolated as I am in the world is there's no one to turn to. I'm an island, no friends, no similarly-aged sister, not even a mother to confide anything in. I bottle it all up, because there's no place else for anything to go.

"How'd you meet him?"

I don't even *like* her, but God, do I want to tell her.

"What's he look like?" she tries again, a lightness to her voice as she tries to coax me into girl talk.

I finally turn to look at her and she brightens, thinking I'm going to spill like she's my girlfriend and we're on a joyous trip to the mall.

Instead I ask, "Why did you keep my bedroom the way I left it?"

The light goes right out of her face. For a minute, I don't think she'll answer, so I lay my head back against the glass.

"I don't know," she finally says. "I guess… it felt like I couldn't lose that part of you, even if I lost the rest."

She says it like I'm the bad guy and she's the victim. Poor her, losing her daughter. I roll my eyes and don't ask anything more.

When we get to the store, I'm already exhausted. I didn't have much energy to begin with, but just the car ride with her zapped me of what little energy I'd mustered.

As we pass racks of men's clothing, I see a fitted black shirt that reminds me of Liam. I don't think about it, I certainly don't intend to, but as we pass it I reach out and caress the front.

My mom gives me a side eye and looks back over her shoulder at the shirt. "Pretty shirt."

"Yeah."

"Does he wear shirts like that?"

"Paul?" I ask, deliberately oblivious. "No."

Just the thought of Paul in a shirt like that makes me want to retch.

"No, I—what's his name? I feel silly not knowing."

"Why would you?" I reply, and walk a little faster, hoping to leave her behind.

But she doesn't give up. "Because I'm your mother. You were a *teenager* the last time you talked to me about a boy you liked."

Yeah, before your husband killed my dad—go figure.

I don't say it, but I'm sorely tempted to.

"We don't have that kind of relationship anymore," I say, because it's just easier.

"Well, maybe I don't think that's fair."

I scoff, but I really don't want to get into it with her. I don't have the energy, and if I did, it wouldn't be in front of shoppers at the mall.

"Let's just get a dress and get this over with," I tell her.

She's unimpressed with my attitude but I'm unimpressed with the whole of life, so I win.

Eventually we make our way to the pretty dresses. I used to like dresses, but I never wear them anymore. Still, it's not torture to slide the hangers down the racks, searching for that perfect dress.

In my mind, in my dumb, stupid, idiot mind, I picture wearing one for Liam. Without ever having seen that man decked out in a sharp suit or button down and slacks, I'd bet everything I own he would look like a dream. I picture a different life, one where we were free to be together, and Paul, I don't know... perished in a soggy condom on the end of his father's dick, and I'm loved and protected by the stoic stranger who pinned me up against my tree.

There's no version of that life, I imagine. How would I have ever met Liam if not for all this?

I don't even know what he *does*, exactly. He seems like a soldier, but I seriously doubt he's any kind of Mafia if he's working for Raj. Private security, maybe. Former military. He has the build and posture for it.

I want to know so much more about him. I want to know everything. Does he have sisters? Are his parents alive? Does he snore? What did he want to be when he grew up? Probably not whatever he is, but maybe. I just want to know.

And I never will.

That's so depressing that all the dresses are suddenly ugly, their looks withered with my mood.

"What about this one?" my mom asks, lifting a Barbie pink dress with rhinestones.

I blink. "Mom, no."

"It's pretty!"

My eyes go wide and I just turn and walk away, because there's nothing else to be done about that situation.

I find a rack of black dresses much more suited to my mood but my mother comes over and glares at me like I've massacred a litter of kittens until I finally give up and walk away from them.

After the Barbie dress, I don't have a lot of faith in my mom picking a dress I'll like, so a moment later when she says, "Oh, this is lovely," I'm not expecting much.

But it is.

The dress she holds up is deep red satin with black straps. The bust is adorned with rhinestones, but it looks elegant, not like the Barbie dress. I have a hunch my boobs will look great in it, and I want Liam to see me in it, because maybe then the bastard would actually want to bang me.

I'm pretty sure I'd look bangable in that dress. I pluck it from my mom's hand and look at it from all angles, the front and the back. "I'll try this one on."

She's proud of herself, but I don't hold that against the dress.

Standing in the dressing room mirror, I admire my reflection. I didn't try this morning when it came to hair or make-up—ratty bun, what is this make-up you speak of?—but the dress twinkles in the light and I love it.

I emerge with the dress hanging over my arm. My mom waits on my verdict, and I offer a satisfied nod.

She claps—actually claps, just once, but she still did it—and lets out a little, "Ha!" but I ignore her. I'm so pleased with the dress I even smile a little, but with my back to my mom so she doesn't see it.

Before we leave, she hauls me into the 'intimates' for a new bra and panty set to go with the dress. I don't know why she bothers, since I have to attend the party with Paul, but given the cut of the dress I'm not positive that any of my bras will actually work, so I allow it. I end up having to try the dress on again over several black bras. The V is really deep and it takes quite a few tries before we find one that works.

I'm tempted to take a picture in the dressing room to send to the number Liam gave me, but I haven't used it, and to be honest, I'm not sure if it's even a cell phone number. The last thing I need is to send a sexy picture to a rotary phone or something, and I'd take his silence as yet another rejection.

I don't want to think about that. Not his rejection or the fact that, in our actual lives, there's no way of anything working between us. At all.

I may as well be a princess in love with a goddamn toad, for all that he's available to me.

Or maybe I'm the toad.

Shaking off thoughts of ill-fitting fairy tales, I take off the dress and head outside, relieved that this whole shopping excursion is over and I can finally go home and climb into bed.

CHAPTER TWELVE
Annabelle

After the shopping excursion, I'm hit with a depressive state. Another cloudy chunk of time where I don't leave my bed, but the sun rises and sets for everyone else.

I think it's the third or fourth day when I feel like getting up.

Paul doesn't come home that night, but now that I'm paranoid about the house being bugged, it doesn't feel much more relaxing. Initially I thought, no, when would they have bugged the house? I'm literally always here.

But then I remembered the sudden invitation to dinner. We were out of the house all evening. If they started following me after that, they would've had a perfect opportunity to come into my house while Paul and I were over at my mother's.

So maybe my house is bugged. That's fun.

When I emerge from my sleep cave, I find the house a mess.

Paul has been home each night I've stayed in bed, so dishes are piled up in the sink and the kitchen smells sour. Empty Sprite and beer cans litter the countertop (the garbage can is just so far away) and there's an ashtray full of ashes on the coffee table in the living room.

He's smoking again?

I'm more aggravated by the fact that he smoked in the house than anything else. When we first moved in, Paul was a smoker, and I was very adamant that if he wanted to keep up with that disgusting habit, he could smoke in the driveway.

I thought he quit over a year ago, but I guess I haven't really been paying much attention to his habits.

I spend the day cleaning. Sweeping and mopping and doing dishes. There's a rust stain on the sink from a pan he shouldn't have left soaking in water. I even open the window above the sink even though it's really chilly outside, because I need to get the sour smell out.

Some woodland creatures to help out would be nice.

I get everything cleaned and take a shower, but it just makes me think of Liam. I close my eyes and imagine his hands on my breasts, his rough thumbs swiping across my nipples. In my fantasy, he bends to take one and then the other into his mouth, and before I know it, I'm a sexually frustrated mess.

Since I'm in the safety of my shower, I let my hand wander down between my legs, and I imagine his much larger fingers pushing inside me. My other hand caresses my breast, like his would, and I give myself the orgasm he didn't.

My body feels better afterward, but overall it just makes me sad.

I want Liam.

I can't have Liam.

I could've at least had Liam for a few minutes, but Liam pulled back.

I turn my thoughts off before I wind up back in bed.

I decide to go for a walk, more because I want to see if I can figure out who's following me than because I actually want to freeze my ass off. I imagine whoever it is out there scrambling, unsure what to do. Am I going to meet someone? How will they keep an eye on me? They can't walk with me. If I see the same car passing me over and over, I'm bound to think something is up.

Paul calls when I've made it a block away, and Paul never calls me, so I'm severely unimpressed with their stealth skills.

"What are you up to?" he asks, his tone all droopy and lame.

"Going for a walk," I reply.

"Why?"

"Because I felt like it?"

"Oh. Well, I wanted to call to let you know I won't be home tonight."

Like that's something new. He's only ever let me know he wouldn't be home a handful of times—he usually just doesn't show. But I know what this is. His guy told him I left the house and they wanted to find out why. I guess that answers the question of whether or not Paul knows.

"I'll be home tomorrow, but not until dinner time," he tells me.

"Okay," I drawl.

"Maybe you could run to the grocery store tomorrow," he says. "There's no food in the house, and if you felt like making dinner tomorrow, that would be pretty great. Maybe you could make your ziti."

I weigh the idea, rocking my head side to side. "Maybe." I do enjoy a good ziti.

"Cool, thanks."

"I don't have any money." There's like $3 in my purse.

"I left a twenty in the bill envelope in case you needed it."

That's surprisingly thoughtful, but I don't say so. "All

right."

He stays on the phone for a bit longer, but neither of us has anything to say. I want to look around for the guy, but I can't very well turn around and start looking or they'll know I suspect something.

Finally I say, "So, I'm gonna go."

He doesn't argue but I can tell by the way he drags out his goodbye he'd like to stay on the phone.

When I hang up, anger spikes through my stomach. Motherfucker. That stupid asshole is having me followed. Of all the hypocritical *bullshit* he could pull….

I've lost count of all the mistresses he's had over the years—because I've been relieved rather than resentful, like an actual wife—but the first time he thinks I'm into another guy, I have the goddamn mafia literally watching my house for him to come.

Stupid misogynistic asswipes.

I wonder if Liam has driven by to check on me.

I walk for a long time because it's the first taste of freedom I've had lately, but eventually I have to go home. I glance in the windows of the cars parked on the side of the road as I make my way back, but there's nobody in any of them.

The following day, as expected, I wake up alone.

Since Paul put the idea of ziti in my mind, and since I have an appetite, I decide to go to the store to get the ingredients I need to throw it together. It's another nice, cold day, so it'll be a good day to have the oven on. Maybe I'll curl up on the couch with a book and a blanket while it cooks.

The day turns out even cooler than I expected, and by the time I get to the grocery store there's a lovely, light snowfall catching on my hair and coat. It boosts my mood and I'm feeling pretty good as I peruse the aisles.

"Annabelle?"

I'm just about to reach for a pair of bananas. I pause and turn toward the female voice that doesn't ring any bells, and I'm surprised to see my old friend Bethany. In high school we were good friends, but after I 'married' Paul and she went off to college, we lost touch.

"Bethany, hi."

She does that thing where she grabs my shoulders and looks me over, all bright-eyed and normal. I don't love being touched, but I don't say anything.

"Wow, you look *great!*" She sounds surprised, but maybe I'm just not used to the decibel of her voice anymore. God, she's perky.

Much more subdued, I offer a smile. "Thanks, so do you."

"Wow, it's been—God, I don't even—has it been ten years? We can't be that old!"

I smile and my gaze drops to her shopping cart. Empty, except for her purse.

She's touching me again, tapping me on the arm, and my gaze moves back to her face. "Hey, I have a wild idea."

"Oh yeah?"

"Let's grab lunch. We haven't seen each other in so long, we probably have so much catching up to do. I was just thinking about you the other day!"

I don't want to say I only have enough money to buy the groceries I need for dinner and this pair of bananas. Before I can, she's looping her arm around me and giving me a hug that I make terribly awkward by not returning it.

She seems a bit ruffled, but otherwise undeterred. "Come on," she says, nodding her head toward the door. "Do you have anywhere you have to be? Let me buy you lunch."

Well, hell, if she's buying.

I insist on driving separately, because I need a few minutes to recover from her enthusiasm before I can stand to sit across from her and endure more of it. I feel a little guilty, because I know I used to be a brighter person myself, but Jesus, I wasn't this fucking cheerful.

By the time we get to the restaurant, I've recharged a bit. I'm not used to socializing anymore, so I'm not sure I'll be much good at it, but I'd like to try. I don't have friends, but she used to be my friend, so who knows? I was just thinking when I went out with my mom how nice it would be to have an actual friend to talk to. Someone removed from all this bullshit.

Someone like Bethany.

Securing her purse in the spare seat beside her, Bethany looks up at me, beaming. "How *are* you?"

Still following social norms, even though it isn't the truth, I reply, "I'm good. How are you?"

She begins to prattle on about how good she is, about her fiancé and his dog and the romantic hiking trip they went on when he asked her to marry him. I nod and smile politely, but dread creeps up on me at the prospect of her asking me similar questions.

And then she does.

"What about you?" she asks, and I can tell she'd tap my arm again if not for the table between us. I absently give the table an approving pat. "You got married, didn't you?"

I feel myself clamming up. "Yeah."

I don't know how to talk about my marriage, since it's not real and certainly not normal. There's no romantic proposal story, no highlight reel, no epic, hormone-induced love story responsible for me 'marrying' so young. My story isn't the kind you tell an acquaintance over coffee, or lunch, or anything less than a bucket of stiff drinks so no one has to remember it come morning.

She catches sight of my ring finger. I'm still wearing my ruby ring (just in case I end up having to leave in a hurry, on account of someone maybe trying to kill me) but no wedding ring.

And then I have an idea. To be free, if only for the next hour.

"It didn't work out."

She offers a sympathetic grimace. "Oh, I'm sorry to hear that."

But I'm feeling lighter already and I wave it off. "Oh, don't be. It was for the best. Never should've gotten married in the first place. Oh well."

She nods and the waitress comes over to get our drink order. Bethany goes off on a tangent explaining to me how she's doing a green tea cleanse and they don't *have* green tea, so she'll just have water. I'm not sure if a green tea cleanse allows eating out at a restaurant, but she's prattling on about how Becky lost eight pounds doing it, and I don't think she needs to lose eight pounds, but maybe she does.

I remember her being a nervous talker, now that I think about it. Just on and on and on about anything that pops into her mind. I try to be less antisocial and intimidating to make her more comfortable, but I just find myself smiling a lot in the attempt.

After the waitress brings our drinks and takes our meal order, Bethany circles back with what I think is a playful smile.

"*So*, is there a special man in *your* life?"

I feel so awkward, because I don't know how to talk about this anymore either. I bite down on my lower lip and take a drink. My heart is oddly racing, and it feels forbidden and dangerous to talk about Liam, but this is the perfect chance.

"Yeah, sort of," I say.

"Oh!" She's delighted, grinning like the Cheshire Cat. "Tell me everything. Tell me all about him. What's his name?"

There's no reason I shouldn't, and no reason to feel uneasy, but there's something about her enthusiasm that bothers me. It feels familiar and foreign at the same time. It reminds me of my mother when we went dress shopping, trying to lure me into girl talk.

I realize I've been quiet for too long when she asks another question, since I don't seem to be answering that one.

"How'd you meet him?" she asks.

Her smile has weakened at this point and I'm quiet for even longer, so it becomes awkward.

She forces another smile and starts fiddling with her phone on the table.

The sight of her phone clears my mind for a moment, because I can't believe I'm just thinking of this.

She has a phone.

I can't call Liam from mine because they can check it, but no one would ever think to check Bethany's.

Noticing my stare, she lifts the phone, flips it over. "Like it? I just upgraded to this new one yesterday, so I'm still learning all the new features."

I drag my gaze from the phone to look at her. "Can I use your phone?"

Her excitement spikes again. "Yeah, of course!" She pushes it across the table, but I'm still looking at her face, because something feels wrong. She's too excited. Why is she this excited? I'm making her feel uncomfortable and not answering her questions. There's something in her eyes, something that isn't excitement, and I don't know exactly what it is. Is she nervous?

A chill settles over me and I sink against the back cushion of the booth.

Her smile falters and all that's left for a split second is the nervousness. She recovers the smile quickly, but it's too late.

I don't trust her anymore.

My gaze moves away from her and out the pane of glass in the window. There are too many cars and I would never be able to finger the person or people following me anyway, but I can't help looking.

I look back at Bethany, and she's still waiting for me to take her goddamn phone.

"Is everything okay?" she asks.

Her smile looks fake to me now. Maybe I'm just being paranoid, but since my house is being watched, maybe I'm not.

"Fine," I say half-heartedly.

She glances pointedly at her phone. "I need to go to the bathroom anyway, I'll give you a little privacy."

She winks and scoots out of the booth. Once I'm satisfied she's not lingering, I pick up her phone and swipe it open. I touch the phone icon, but instead of making a call, I check her call log. Empty. That's not too weird, given she just told me she upgraded to this phone yesterday, but then I swipe over to contacts and that's empty, too.

Like her cart at the grocery store.

I go back to the numbers and my eyes dance across the ones that comprise Liam's memorized phone number.

I can't call him, because whether it's paranoia or it isn't, my instincts are telling me this is a trap.

I dial numbers anyway, but they're mine. In my purse, my own cell phone rings and I ignore the call. I just want her phone number.

I check over my shoulder again, then I call the number on my cell and wait impatiently until it goes to voice mail. I don't know how long she'll be in the bathroom, and I don't want to get caught checking up on her.

"Hi, you've reached Bethany's phone! I can't answer right now, but leave a message or shoot me a text and I'll get back to you as soon as I can. Have a nice day!" I hang up before it starts recording, then I go into the call log in her phone and erase the calls I just made so it's empty again.

Placing the phone back on the table, I stare at it.

What if I'm being crazy? What if Bethany just has a new phone and hasn't transferred her old stuff over, and she's just nervous and excited because we're old friends but I'm weird now? What if I'm squandering the only chance I'll get to reach out to Liam without anyone knowing I did?

But what if I'm not?

When Bethany comes back, she asks how my call went. I tell her I remembered after she walked away he wasn't on lunch yet. I'm tempted to fill her up with all the answers she wants, but all of them lies. I want to, just to waste everyone's time, but if I do that and she *is* in league with Pietro or Paul or whoever the fuck is doing this, then they'll know I suspect something.

"You weren't planning to meet him for lunch, were you? I hope I didn't ruin your plans."

I smile benignly and shake my head. "Nope."

"Well, when does he go on lunch? You can always try again after, all this water goes straight to my bladder," she says on a laugh.

I offer another bland smile but her continued interest in my use of her phone is alarming. And wouldn't a normal person with no vested interest wonder why I need to use her phone, why I can't use my own?

I wish I could just leave, but that would probably look suspicious, too. I don't want to alert these assholes that I'm onto them.

The most alarming thought is that if Liam wouldn't have told me they were watching my house, I wouldn't be.

I would've taken this opportunity to tell someone about Liam. To reach out to him. Just like someone wanted me to.

CHAPTER THIRTEEN
Annabelle

I make the ziti.

I'm angry so I don't want to, but I don't want to tip anyone off. At least I feel like I have the upper hand if I know something they don't.

The whole night passes uneventfully. Part of me wants to signal Liam somehow so I can warn him that they're going to frankly unprecedented lengths to catch him, but signaling him would increase their chances of doing just that, so I don't.

It's the most depressing thought I've had lately, but I think the best thing I can do for him is leave him alone. It's the last thing I want to do, but since nothing good can come of it and even stolen moments risk him getting hurt or killed, it is the best thing.

He can't protect me, but maybe I can protect him. Liam would've never gotten tangled up in this mess to begin with if not for my sojourn to the apple tree.

Another day passes, then two. The only thing that changes is we're that much closer to my mother's stupid anniversary party. The pretty dress hangs in my closet, never to be seen by the man I want. The man I'll never see again.

I lapse into sadness and stay in bed for a couple of days. Paul doesn't come home, so there's nothing to interrupt me.

I'm out of bed by the time he finally does, but not terribly energized. He looks tired, too.

I didn't make dinner. I'm not hungry and I didn't know he'd be here, and honestly, it's not like knowing would've changed things.

He sighs irritably and tosses his keys across the counter. I glance in his direction, but remain curled up in the cozy chair with my blanket wrapped around me.

Raking an aggravated look at me as he walks past, he says, "You could turn up the goddamn heat, you know."

I don't respond. It's nothing new, but it infuriates him.

"I'm fucking talking to you," he barks.

Dimly aware that this isn't going in a great direction, I glance at him, but I don't have the energy to care, and if I did, I wouldn't waste it on that.

When I don't respond, he tries again to start something. "You wanna make some dinner?"

"There's a frozen pizza in the freezer," I inform him.

"I don't want a frozen fucking pizza."

"Well, we don't have anything else."

I mean, we do, if I felt like making shit from scratch, but that's not going to happen.

"Then go to the goddamn grocery store," he snaps, glaring at me. "That's your job, isn't it? We don't have food? Go buy it."

"That requires money." And leaving the house.

He turns red and storms over, grabbing my blanket.

I hold onto it, because fuck him.

He mutters and swears at me as he tries to pull it away, and I hold on until I'm afraid the fabric's going to tear. By the time he wrestles it away from me, I've fallen from the chair into the floor. He whips the blanket across the room and it falls over the arm of the couch. From my hands and knees I push myself up, but he grabs me, spinning me and backing me up aggressively, then shoving me. I land on the couch, so it's not a hard landing, but I'm not sure what's coming.

It's weird, because his eyes don't look right. He doesn't look enraged when he attacks me, strangled with impotent anger and lashing out. Even the shove felt a little half-hearted.

"What?" he says, as if egging me on.

I don't take the bait. I don't feel like fighting tonight. I just duck to the side and stand, then go to walk past him so I can get the frozen pizza out.

He stops me, grabbing me again, shoving me against the counter. It does hurt when my hip slams against the edge of the counter, but I don't show it. He grabs a chunk of my hair and yanks, and it hurts my heart instead of my head. Liam in the woods with his hand fisted in my hair right before he kisses me flashes across my mind.

Ouch.

A slap across the face pulls me out of my Liam memory, but it's not as hard as I expect it to be.

"What are you gonna do, huh?" he asks. "You gonna call your fucking boyfriend?"

I meet his eyes then, his half-hearted, not all that angry eyes, and it clicks—he wants me to.

My gaze jerks to the front windows. I don't know if I expect to see shadowy figures, poised to take him down when he shows, but I don't.

"Huh?" he says again, jerking my chin so I'm looking at him again. "You think I'm afraid of him?"

I don't know what's going on, but I'm placid as I meet his gaze. "I think all of you are."

Something jumps in his eyes, and that's not anger either. My mind races to string together the pieces, to keep up.

The rage he mustered seems to drain right out of him. He stays close, holding onto my arm, but there's no force now.

"What?" he says, in case he misunderstood.

"Why do you want me to call him?"

He tries to say, "I don't want you to call him…" but I shake my head, fed up.

"Bullshit. What the hell is going on?"

He drops my arm now and backs up, his pretense of anger evaporated. He sighs, dropping his head into his hands and swearing.

"Why do you have to be so goddamn difficult?" he finally mutters.

I follow him down on the couch and wait.

Finally he looks up, after a few more dramatic sighs, and says, "You need to tell me where you met this guy. For real."

"Nope. Next."

"Annabelle… I'm serious."

"Why?"

"Because I'm pretty sure he's using you," he states.

My stomach drops but my face remains impassive. It's a stupid thing to say and I'm angry at him for even saying it, but I want to hear his reasoning.

"If you're not going to say anything…" Paul trails off.

"Why would you even think that?"

"Quite a few reasons. Things are going on, things you don't know about."

I instantly shoot back, "What things?"

"I can't tell you that." He shakes his head very slightly. "Things. Bad things. Things that shouldn't be happening. It seems like someone's…" He evades again, shaking his head. His gaze flits up, toward the ceiling, then abruptly falls. "Just trust me on this, okay? Bad shit. Bad for *us*. I think that guy has something to do with it."

I have no idea what he's talking about or if it's possible Liam *does* have anything to do with it, and I'm aggravated by the vagueness. "Well, if you can't tell me anything, why should I tell you anything?"

"How did you even happen across this guy? He approached you, I assume?"

I stand, shaking my head. "If you can't tell me—"

He stands too, grabbing my arm and jerking me back, but this time not in a forced show of aggression. Desperation seeps out of him.

"How did he fucking find you?"

I get chills again, trying to break his grasp, but his words are actually starting to get to me.

Liam didn't come out of nowhere, and he isn't the one who approached me, but what is Raj doing that he's so worried about me finding out about? That warranted having me followed home, to make sure… what had Liam said? That I didn't report back to Pietro?

What would I report back to Pietro for?

"What kind of stuff is going wrong?" I ask again.

Frustration etched plainly on his face, he swears again, but this time it smells of surrender. "I can't… Some stuff was stolen."

"Stuff?"

"Don't worry about it. It's not just that either, it's… that guy doesn't fight like a normal guy. He doesn't fight like a *civilian*," he says pointedly.

My eyes roll of their own volition. "I wouldn't call him throwing you off the bed and stepping on your throat a *fight*, Paul."

His face reddens. "Not that night. Before that, before I knew who he was. The night at the bar."

Now I frown. I don't mean to, I probably shouldn't have, but I don't know what he's talking about and I'm caught unawares. He immediately registers that and starts nodding in a knowing way that makes me immediately regret the slip.

"He didn't tell you. You don't know."

"What?" I snap, defensive.

"Remember when I came home with the black eye? He was at the bar that night. When I went outside to leave, he picked a fight with me."

I smirk and though I want to remark on how Liam sure didn't look like *he'd* been in a fight, I hold my tongue.

My smirk doesn't bother him though and he says, "Tell me something, Annabelle. If the guy's into you, what was he doing following *me*?"

I quickly try to reconcile the timeline in my mind, but I lose days a lot and I'm not immediately sure when that happened. Doesn't slow my reply though.

"Hm, I don't know, do you think it might have something to do with the fact that I have an abusive partner? He probably wanted to punch you in the face for hurting me."

It pisses Paul off and I have no idea if that's true, but it does sound nice in my head.

"Wake the fuck up, Annabelle," he practically spits. "He doesn't give a fuck about you. He's *using* you to get to us."

The junkyard comes to mind again and though my mind

almost never sides with Paul, doubt creeps in. Is it even remotely possible Paul's right? Frankly, if Liam *did* want to use me to hurt Paul or my stepfather, I'd probably let him. That would bring me joy, too. But the idea of him fooling me into it certainly rubs the wrong way.

"What do you think he stole?" I ask.

"That's not the point." He's getting worked up, for real this time. Apprehension grips me but I ignore it. "Don't you fucking get it, Annabelle? He's *using* you. He doesn't *care* about you! You don't mean *shit* to him."

Ooookay, that's what this is.

He wants to hurt me. He *needs* me to be hurt by this reveal.

He's hurt by my interest in a man, finally—but not him. Why would it be him? But he would never consider that, obviously. I'm the asshole, I should love him; off with my head.

I even consider letting him think he's got me. Oh no, my lover is using me! Woe is fucking me. Not like I've ever been *used* by a dickhead or two before.

In the end, I can't. It goes against my nature to let him get one over on me, even if it's just pretend.

Smiling faintly, I say, "So?"

His eyes about bulge out of his head. "What the fuck do you mean, so? He's manipulating you. You're a fucking pawn to him, a means to an end—"

I interrupt. "Well, it sounds like you've got it all figured out, so I don't know what you need me for. Who cares what his name is or how I met him or anything else? You seem to know all about what he's capable of and what his motivations are. Me? I'm just a clueless little pawn."

He's pissed now, for real, so he grabs me and shoves me against the wall. "Did you know? Huh? D'you know he's pulling some shit on your own goddamn husband? Your own goddamn family? Are you in on it?"

He's not even making sense, but there's no point trying to reason with him. Pain radiates through my elbow as he slams me against the wall again and it hits at just the right angle. He turns me until I'm belly-up against the wall and he crowds me, pushing his body against my back.

"You think that's cute, huh? You think you're making a fool out of me?"

I smile but he can't see it so I laugh.

"What's fucking funny?" he booms.

"That you imagine I actually think about you when I'm with him," I taunt.

A low growl emanates from his throat and a lump of fear forms in mine, but fuck it. Hopelessness rears its ugly head, reminding me I'll probably never even see Liam again, and what am I even doing all of this for?

At least I get a moment of pleasure at the sinking feeling I must've given Paul before his hands are suddenly bouncing my head off the wall, causing my vision to waver.

I push back, but I'm trying to get my vision oriented and it makes me vulnerable. He pushes me and I fall to my knees, only catching myself on one arm. Little white clouds of nothing have me all foggy, but I know the mechanics, so I rely on muscle memory to get back to my feet.

May have worked, if Paul wasn't there to push me back down.

I'm still in pajama pants, and they're easy for him to pull down.

"No," I snap, grabbing them, pulling until they rip. Goddammit. I kick at him and he sits on my legs, creeping up my body, yanking his belt off. I'm not sure if he plans to fuck me or whip me with the belt, and I'm not even sure which outcome I prefer.

Well, none.

Gripped by an idea, I retreat.

"Paul, please."

He likes that. Fucker likes me begging.

"Oh, yeah, you're a big, bad bitch now, huh?" he taunts, tossing his belt aside with relish.

He thinks I'm relenting, begging, soft, so he isn't as guarded as he should be, isn't prepared for it when I twist as if in defense and suddenly bring my knee up. It's not easy and I have to fight and scratch and kick like hell, but I manage to knee him in the junk. While he's reacting, I bring my feet up and kick him off me.

"You little fucking cunt," he screams, his voice high.

My heart hammers as I launch to my feet, catching my balance on the wall and bounding down the hall to the bedroom.

I look to the window, wishing Liam was out there. I want to be saved. I want help. I don't want to have to do this alone.

But he isn't, and I am alone, but for the one advantage Paul doesn't know I have.

I make it to my bedside table and jerk it open, quickly finding the stun gun Liam gave me. I don't know what I'm doing, haven't had a chance to think through the ramifications. All I know is that motherfucker isn't going to win tonight.

He bounds down the hallway like a bat out of hell and throws open the bedroom door. A sick, smug smile plays on his thin little lips.

I'm doubting myself and my ability to even use this damn stun gun. Paul isn't the strongest of men, certainly no match for Liam, but he is stronger than me. He hasn't seen it yet, but what if he's able to disarm me?

"You're pathetic," he says, shaking his head as he steps inside.

This is funny, coming from him.

"It must have been so easy for him to prey on you. The boss' sad, lonely stepdaughter. You must've been so fucking *desperate* for the attention, the *connection*. He saw a means to an end and bonus sex; you saw a motherfucking soulmate."

It feels like an ice cube slides through my body but I don't show a reaction.

"So fucking unloved. You must've been so fucking easy. All he had to do was be *nice* to you."

I wish I could kill him. I can't even stop my lip from curling up, momentarily overcome with hatred for the sad, angry little man before me. I want to scream at him, claw his face off, remind him that *he's* the one who made me like this.

But I'll be damned if I ever give him the satisfaction of thinking he has that kind of power over me.

Or any of them. I hate all of them in that moment, more intensely than I have in a long time.

Because he's right.

Maybe not in actuality, maybe he's not right about whatever Liam's doing, but he's right about that.

I was easy. I was lonely. If Liam *did* want to seduce me to get to my family, they sure as hell groomed me for it.

They stole my life.

They carved out the person I once was and left me a goddamn shell.

I want to say something awful to him, something truly scathing, but I'm too overcome by resentment and a massive headache to come up with anything.

My fingers flex on the stun gun he still hasn't seen, hidden behind my leg. I'll die before I let him put his hands on me tonight, and I don't know where I'll go or what I'll do or how far from the house I'll even make it afterward, but by God, tonight I will fight to the death.

I'm ready.

Maybe that's why he fades. Maybe he can sense it. Maybe his balls just hurt because of my attack, I don't know. But he doesn't come any closer. He shakes his head, giving me a mean look that might hurt if I gave even half a damn.

"Fuck you," he says, still shaking his head. Then he spits on the ground, meeting my gaze. "I don't even fucking want you anymore."

And with that, he turns and leaves.

CHAPTER FOURTEEN
Liam

As I bite into my cold chicken sandwich, an envelope drops onto the cheap folding table in front of me.

I pause mid-chew and put the sandwich down, grabbing the envelope, thick with cash, and thumbing through it.

Upon verification that it's the sum I expected, I put it back down and resume eating my sandwich.

"Your bonus," Raj says, in case I hadn't pieced that shit together.

"Half my bonus," I correct him.

Chuckling lightly, he says, "Of course. I would never dream of cheating you."

"I should hope not."

"The other half when the job is done, naturally."

I don't respond, but he lingers, seeming to want me to.

"A gesture of good faith, if you will," he continues.

He's nervous.

I put the sandwich down and turn in my seat so I can look up at him. "Is there something you need, or can I finish my lunch?"

Most people aren't so direct and he's momentarily surprised. He recovers quickly enough, pulling out the chair next to me and taking a seat. He removes his glasses, gently squeezing the bridge of his nose, and then puts them back.

"I realize it's not exactly my business what you do once your contract is up, but I was wondering if you had any interest in sticking around here."

It's obviously a question, but he doesn't make it sound like one. My mind jumps to Annabelle, the only reason I would have any interest in sticking around, but he hasn't mentioned the idea of bringing her over to his side again, and I don't want him to know she's still on my mind.

I shake my head, a wordless no.

He nods, but disappointment flits across his features. "I was thinking… if you were looking for something a little more permanent, maybe I could use a guy like you."

I'm not interested, not even a little bit, but I am curious, so I don't immediately say so. "How do you mean? Protection?"

"No. Well… not precisely. A sort of protection." He looks at me, trying to read me or something, but it doesn't work, so he remains tentative. "After all is said and done and Pietro's empire is toppled, there will be new opportunities, a very brief window before someone else comes into power. Money to be made." He's watching me for interest as he speaks, and I get the impression he's holding back, but I'm also not dense, so I can fill in the pieces myself.

I cock my head slightly, but my face betrays nothing of my thoughts. "I thought this was about avenging your son."

Scowling fiercely, he says, "This *is* about my son. Of course it is."

I nod once, accepting his word for it.

I understand. It may be about vengeance, but Raj is an opportunist and the situation he's creating is too great to pass up. He wants to take advantage of the chaos after the fall, and he needs muscle.

"Well, I like being a freelancer; I'm not looking for anything permanent," I tell him.

"It wouldn't have to be *permanent*. Just another job after you complete this one."

I look at him and flash him a smile. "After this one, I'm taking a vacation."

He looks disappointed. "I see. Well, if you change your mind...."

"I won't."

Raj stands and goes to leave, but after only a couple of steps, I hear his footsteps pause. I'm more alert, shoulders tensing. Ordinarily I'm not this tense doing a job, but ordinarily I don't fuck around and catch feelings for the people involved. I can't shake the feeling of being a double agent when I'm around Raj, or the concern that he might start to see that.

I half expect to be jumped several times a day at this point, whether at work, or when I show up back at the place I'm calling home right now. Raj's guy or one of Pietro's? Who fucking knows anymore. It's no way to live.

"It's important that the entire family be removed," Raj finally says.

I don't react, but he's obviously talking about Annabelle. It makes me uneasy that he's even bringing this up again, that he thinks I'm still worried about her.

He can't trust me if he thinks that.

I can't rely on him if he doesn't know he can rely on me.

I wanna hurl my half eaten sandwich across the goddamn

room. This is *exactly* why this sort of shit shouldn't happen. Needless complications. This job was stressful enough before Annabelle had to pick her goddamn apples.

Back to the task at hand, I drop my sandwich and stand, turning to face Raj. I can tell by the step he takes backward that he's afraid of me, and not just in the way you *should* be afraid of someone you've paid to help you kill an entire mob family.

Jumpier than that.

The kind of fear that makes a man unpredictable.

I turn back and pick up the envelope on the table, holding it out to him.

He frowns at the envelope, startled. "What…?"

"If you're questioning my ability to see this job through, I can't work for you anymore," I tell him, simply.

Startled shifts to alarmed and his dark eyes go wide. "No! No, I… I wasn't questioning you, Liam."

"It sure sounds like you were, and I don't believe I've given you cause to doubt me. I've done everything you asked of me, every step of the way."

He can't argue that, but it's obviously not as cut and dry as I make it sound. "Annabelle…"

"I don't like men who hit women," I state, implacably, but detached. "I'll be happy to kill her husband. I'd be happy to do it early, slowly, brutally."

I can tell he doesn't want to keep pushing, since, well, I just tried to quit on him right before show time, but he stands his ground, raises his chin, and asks, "And if Annabelle walks out of that house and into your crosshairs?"

"Then she dies," I state.

I say it simply, unemotionally, but not coldly. As if we're discussing a storm on the weather forecast—not ideal, but not something that's going to ruin my life.

He accepts this and looks like a weight has been lifted. "I regret questioning your loyalty."

"It isn't a matter of loyalty," I stated, turning and sitting back down, dropping the envelope full of cash and picking up the sandwich. "You paid me to do a job. The job will get done. Don't insult me again and we'll be fine."

"Of course."

I hear him leave and the space should feel bigger, less constricting. But the walls close in instead. I feel trapped, cornered. Not a feeling I'm accustomed to. Not a feeling I like. I was bluffing when I tried to give him back his money—I figure he can't replace me at this point if he hasn't already—but I can't shake disappointment that he didn't take me up on it. I'm making a lot of money on this job, but I'd give it all back if it meant washing my hands of this whole situation and getting the hell out of it.

If it meant going back in time and never meeting Annabelle.

I'm not afraid of her family, but I'm a little afraid of her.

She should be afraid of me, but Annabelle is never afraid when she should be.

I've tried to keep my distance since they've been watching her. *Have* kept my distance. But I still check in.

Now I need to get in.

Paul's home, so I picked a shit time to show up. I can't hang around or I risk drawing attention.

I drive around the neighborhood for a bit, looking for inspiration. I can't get Paul out of the house, but if I go back later, maybe he'll have left for that other chick's bed.

Fucking idiot.

Knowing what I do now about how their "relationship" started, it makes more sense, but Jesus, doesn't he have any fucking game? He couldn't have won her over instead of trying to force her into submission? A couple days with her should've alerted the steaming pile of dogshit that he was taking the wrong approach, let alone a couple months, the first year. Learn to read the room, asshole. I guarantee if *I* was the asshole her stepfather forced her to marry, things would've turned out differently.

Jesus Christ, listen to me. *Marriage*. Ugh.

I wish I could just shoot him without ruining everything. One fucking shot from far away, boom—he's gone.

It's aggravating that I can't. Literally in any other scenario I could just eliminate the obstacle standing in my way.

Fucking Raj.

Fucking mob families.

I wait until later to go back, and when I do, Paul's truck is gone. Less fortunately, it isn't the stupid cell phone fuck guarding her tonight, but the guy who actually watches—and boy, is he watching tonight. I observe him for a few minutes, and I've actually seen him walk along the far side of the house and check the back yard twice in the ten minutes since Paul left.

It's not a risk I want to take, and it's not pressing enough to justify it.

I wish I could walk around back and just peek in her bedroom window, just to see her. The light's on, so she's probably in there.

But it's not worth it. I need to talk to her, and I will, but

Paul's gone a lot. I'll come back tomorrow, and hopefully then it will be the younger kid.

    Tomorrow I will kiss her.

    Tomorrow I will hold her.

    Tomorrow I will warn Annabelle not to go to that goddamn party.

CHAPTER FIFTEEN
Annabelle

"Pack your shit."

I heard Paul rustling around in the closet when he got home, but the weight of something being thrown on top of me as I lay curled up under my blankets gives me a jolt.

I don't understand what he's doing, but I don't have the energy to deal with it. I'm not up to engaging and it shows as I roll over, scowling, then craning to see what he threw at me.

A suitcase.

"What?" I ask, bleary and confused.

He looks tired. Dim. Worn down. Older than last time I took a good, long look at him.

"Get up."

I'm confused, and his words aren't registering. They can't. I don't have the experience to reconcile his actions with his words.

"Why?"

"Because you need to pack. Your. Shit," he says, enunciating slowly, like I'm especially dense.

"Why am I packing my shit?" Still frowning. Still confused. Still not getting it.

He sighs, like I'm being aggravating.

"Come on, Annabelle."

I do sit up, slowly, but I'm still bewildered.

"You're going to stay with your mom," he says.

Fear coils around my gut like a snake, squeezing the breath right out of me. "What? No! No, I'm not."

"You have to. You don't have anywhere else to go," he states, with the sureness of a man who never has his life decided for him.

I don't know what I'm feeling. Well, terror. Terror. I don't want to go. I *can't* go back there.

"Why? Why? Are we going...?"

But I know before I ask, I know. I understand. He's given up on me. It's hard to wrap my head around it, after years of him fighting to hold onto me, of fighting *me*, I never thought I'd live to see the day he willingly released me. I'd fantasized about it a couple of times, but it wasn't realistic so I didn't make it so far as to plan where I would end up if he did.

He doesn't meet my gaze. "Pack your clothes. What you need now, at least. I'll send the rest later."

"You're leaving me." The words sound foreign coming out of my mouth. They sound wrong. He's not my real husband and I don't want anything to do with him...

But he's all I have.

Without him, without anything of my own, I'm at the mercy of my mother. I picture myself packing up a suitcase and being hauled over to my old house (I don't imagine I'll be allowed to keep my car). Trudging up the steps of my old home, pushing open the squeaky door of my old bedroom, and being stuck there. Helpless. Even more helpless than I am here, and surrounded by everything that makes me feel sick.

I hear a wheezing noise, and it takes a minute to realize it's coming from me. I can't breathe. My chest feels thick, closing in more by the second, and I'm sick to my stomach. I try to breathe but I've waited too late and I'm panicking.

Paul mutters a curse and sits on the edge of the bed, but he doesn't know what to do.

"I can't," I gasp out, desperation clawing at my insides and seeping out of my goddamn eyeballs. Years of concealing my fear and this, this is the moment I lose control. When the motherfucker kicks me out.

Unsure whether I'm saying I can't, as in I can't breathe, or objecting to moving back in with my awful mother and the suffocating feelings my childhood home stirs in me, Paul stands, paces, grabs his cell phone like he's going to call someone, but then looks to me for direction.

Goddammit, he's never been good in a crisis.

I claw at my chest, my fucking aching chest, and it hurts to be trapped inside my brain. I just want out.

I start rocking. I don't try to steady my breathing. My vision is starting to waver on account of no oxygen coming in and lots of desperate, explosive attempts to breathe, and I'm so. Fucking. Helpless.

Tears spring to my eyes but they don't fall. I think. I'm not sure.

Everything gets far away, everything feels so strange, and then everything goes black.

I guess I didn't really pass out.

I don't know, but nobody mentioned it.

I have no memory of what happened after that.

I only have now, sitting on the ugly floral couch at my mother's, running my hands across the coarse fabric, using my index finger to trace the pink rose.

Pretty. It's so pretty.

Wait, it's pretty? I thought it was ugly. I've always hated this couch, haven't I?

Who cares.

I feel light and floaty and only dimly aware of my problems. They're there, somewhere, in the shadows, but I'm so fine, and I need to be fine, so I accept it and don't complain.

I feel myself smile—literally. I bring my fingers to my face and feel my skin stretching. Then I laugh, because... I'm not sure, actually.

Suddenly, my mother is there. I lean back, looking up at her, and my head falls back against the couch, because wow, my head is heavy!

I feel like I'm supposed to say something to her. Ask her something. What was it?

Oh!

"Paul," I say, holding an unsteady hand up. "Where's Paul?"

My mother's face turns sympathetic and she perches on the edge of the couch. Leaning in, she places a hand on my leg and rubs it, as if to comfort me. "Oh, honey."

Oh honey? I don't know, I don't care. I dip forward with my big, heavy head and look at the floor. Pink carpet. Peachy pink. Not the same color as the pink rose I was tracing, but man, it looks so soft I just want to bury my face in it.

So I do.

I fall to my knees on the floor and flatten myself down in one coily movement. I run my fingers across the carpet the same way I did the couch, and everything is so lovely.

I roll over on my back, but I miss the feel of the carpet so I roll over again. I'm a few feet away from my mom now, after all the rolling. I'm back to feeling the carpet, this time with my cheek.

"It's lovely," I tell her.

"Can you come back to the couch?" she asks, gently.

Experimentally I make the attempt, pushing myself up, but my arms don't feel terribly strong while my body feels heavier than a body has a right to.

"How do I walk every day?"

My mom blinks, eyes wide in confusion. "What?"

"My body is so heavy, how do I walk *every day*? It's so heavy. I just…" I trail off, losing interest in what I was saying, and rest my cheek against the carpet.

My mother finally moves off the couch and joins me on the floor. She stays up on her knees, a hand tentatively reaching out to rub my back.

I sigh, content. That feels so nice.

"How are you feeling?" she asks me.

"Everything is lovely," I tell her with another dreamy sigh.

The carpet is so clean. I wonder if anyone ever even comes in this room. Maybe she just vacuums a lot.

Or there's probably a maid. Maybe? I don't know. It doesn't matter, but the carpet is so soft and my face is buried in it again.

"Honey, I need to ask you a few things. Is that okay?"

"Mm hmm," I murmur, petting the carpet.

"Annabelle, honey, pay attention," she says.

"I am," I insist, glancing up at her.

"Okay." She pauses, looking… I don't know. Something.

Then she says, "Do you remember the man you've been... involved with?"

I've turned myself around so I can see under the couch, and I see something under there! Crawling forward on my belly, I reach underneath and fish around. It's clean so I probably don't have to worry about touching anything yucky.

"Annabelle."

A hand is on my shoulder and I roll over on my back, folding my hands across my belly. "Remember when Daddy used to take me to the—"

"Annabelle, I need you to focus," she says, and I realize she's... irritated? Have I done something wrong?

"The man. There's a man, the one who beat up Paul."

Oh *yeah*! I wrinkle my nose up, but without much censure. "Paul. Paul isn't nice."

"Well..."

"Or interesting. Or smart. Poor Paul."

"Annabelle, do you remember a man attacking Paul?"

I frown lightly, reviewing my memory. "Oh, yes! Thor," I say with a dreamy grin.

"Thor?" she asks, alert. "His name is Thor?"

I giggle. "Yeah. He's a superhero. He's really sexy."

"He's not a superhero, honey. That man is a danger to all of us. I need you to tell me more. Where does he live? Have you seen where he lives?"

"Oh, no. Asgard is very far away."

"Asgard," she repeats, jotting something down on a piece of paper I just noticed on her lap. "Is that the name of his apartment complex? Does he live in an apartment?"

I snort and collapse in a fit of laughter, because my mom is so silly. "He protects me. He makes me happy."

She falters, her hand pausing in whatever she's writing. She looks down at me, and a strand of long dark hair has somehow made it in my mouth with the rolling and crawling and long hair. I spit it out, pushing my hair out of my face and staring up at the ceiling.

"I feel a little queasy," I tell her, suddenly aware of a tummy ache.

And then I throw up all over the clean, peachy pink carpet.

"You need to lower the dose."

My eyes are still closed, but I'm aware of my mother's voice—persistent, almost desperate.

"The dose is fine."

"It's too strong," she says. "It shouldn't make her sick."

"That may not have been the medicine," a male voice says, dismissively. Indifferent.

Pietro.

My heart leaps and it's a struggle to keep my eyes closed.

"You didn't see her—she was completely out of it," my mother tells him.

His voice is dry. "Yes, I heard. *Thor*."

I can't see my mother, but her tone sounds defensive. "It could be a code name!"

"It's a fucking Norse God," Pietro returns, slamming something. "Nothing she said is useful."

"We don't even know if he's connected. I'll ask her again, I'll *get* answers, but you need to lower the dose."

I hear his heavy footfall. "She won't talk to you if she's off the meds. Not even about her goddamn superhero boyfriend."

"Not *off* the meds, Pietro, just less. The doctor said...."

I strain to hear what she says, but they've left the room and they're too far down the hall.

I'm afraid to open my eyes. I don't know if I'm alone. I don't want anyone to know I'm awake, because I'm not completely clear on what the actual fuck is happening.

I remember the exchange she referred to. I was high out of my mind, rolling around the floor and eating my own hair. Jesus Christ.

They drugged me? With what?

How long have I been here?

The lack of power over my own body is starting to get to me, so I stop thinking and slow down. Take a few subtle breaths, just in case I'm not alone in the room.

I get my shit together and peek under a shuddering eyelid. Clear.

My eyes open and I look around. I'm not in my bed in my old room. I'm on a cot—I think it's a cot. It's narrow and white and sort of hard. Like a hospital bed. I'm in a lower level spare room, the now-blue one with a nautical painting hanging above the bed.

Why didn't they just put me on the bed?

I look down at my hands and my heart stops. I'm hooked up to something—an IV? There's a needle taped to the top of my left hand, poked into a vein.

Jesus Christ.

Actually, now would be a really great time for some divine intervention, I think, eyes darting to the ceiling. Anyone listening? Hello?

No guardian angel appears and I guess I'm on my own. Against Pietro and drugs and my own mother. In my old house. Guarded, with an alarm and a security system.

Helplessness swallows me whole. I long for the days when Paul was out doing God knows what and I had a safe bed to curl up in. I long for that shred of security, now that I have none.

And I long for Liam to come crashing through the ceiling like an actual fucking superhero and whisk me away.

I close my eyes, not to maintain a pretense of sleep, but to keep in the tears.

I won't cry.

I won't cry.

I'm so tired.

But I have to fight.

Again.

CHAPTER SIXTEEN
Liam

I don't have to hate someone to kill them. I don't need to be able to justify it. I don't operate on the same level most people seem to when it comes to the act of taking a life. It's a thing that has to be done in some cases, just like any other thing. You can't stop eating because you don't want to do dishes. I kill the people who cross someone with enough money to hire out their dirty work.

My next kill will be pro bono. Whichever goon comes between me and Annabelle.

But doing the job for Raj? Oh, I'm going to relish the fuck out of that.

I haven't experienced a lot of strong, moving emotions in my time, but the level of hatred I'm reaching with regards to Annabelle's family….

Well, I'd do the job even if Raj decided not to pay me at this point.

For a minute, a brief fucking minute somewhere along this line, I considered bowing out, out of respect for Annabelle. Even if she didn't like them, even if she had fucked up relationships with them and they wronged her in heinous ways that I, personally, would never forgive, in some part of her soul, they were still her family.

Not anymore.

Now they're just parasites who need exterminating.

That I will do out of respect for Annabelle.

I just have to figure out how the fuck to get her out of their clutches before then. I'm waiting for the opportunity. It's going to come. It has to. They can't keep her locked up in that goddamn fortress forever.

They'll let her out eventually, with a guard of some sort.

They'll take her somewhere. I'll follow. Kill the guard. Take Annabelle. She'll never go back there, and I don't care if it compromises Raj's whole operation at this point. Those who need killing will get theirs, even if I have to storm the goddamn *castle* myself.

But first, Annabelle.

It's hard not to kill Paul as I watch him move that other bitch into Annabelle's house. I understand now, that burning hatred that compels people to hire me. He goes on with his life in a blissful fucking blur, as if Annabelle never even existed, while she's….

I don't even know.

I can't get inside Pietro's house, inside his gates, without detection.

I have no idea what's going on with her.

During the day I have to work for Raj, so maybe that's when they're letting her out and I'm missing it.

I'm running out of time.

The party is in five days. Annabelle doesn't know not to go

to it, and if she's living at the house and not able to leave, it won't even matter.

She can't be in the house.

I don't even know if she's okay.

I don't know if Paul did something to her, broke a limb, maybe? That would explain why she isn't leaving.

There have been moments, gripping, awful moments, where I wonder if she's even alive. I don't entertain them for long, feeling that somehow I would know if she wasn't. A funeral, a burial—goons moving a body out of the house in the middle of the night. Something would happen. And nothing has.

Last night I got desperate. There's no time to wait anymore and I have to know what's going on. I bribed a guy I know at the power company and went up on the poles with him so I could plant a camera to record the comings and goings. If I can figure out when they're letting her leave the house, I'll change my schedule with Raj accordingly. He's getting cagey as the big day draws nearer, but I don't care. In a few days, I'll never see Raj again.

I can't consider the possibility that I won't be able to get to Annabelle before then. I can't blend in with the caterers to get inside—I'm too big, too off; there's an energy I exude that wouldn't work. I'll stand out. Get killed. Fail to rescue Annabelle.

Unacceptable.

If I have to, if I absolutely have to, I'll call in a couple favors of my own. I'll have Lance and Raj taken out. I'll turn. I'll blow the whole operation. And my reputation, most likely.

Even in my head, this is getting messy.

I don't like messy.

I've never been this uncomfortable in my life. Regrets nag at me every night—thoughts of Annabelle by the tree behind her house, kissing me, wanting me.

Why the fuck had I pushed her away?

I should've just taken her then. I could've sent her ahead of me, finished the job, and met up with her afterward. Sure, maybe they would've been alarmed by her disappearance, maybe Raj would've suspected me, but Annabelle would be safe.

That shouldn't be the most important thing to me—shouldn't be my first thought upon waking and the last thought before I finally pass out sometime in the wee hours of the morning.

But it is.

I'm consumed by her.

I want her back in my arms more than I've ever wanted anything in my life, and I'm actually terrified that it will never happen. That I'll lose her, when I never even had her in the first place.

Annabelle is going to be mine. She *is* mine, whether she knows it now or not.

So right now her family is fucking with what's mine.

Bad idea.

I've more or less stopped sleeping, but it's worth it.

Because I'm there when she steps onto the front porch around 3am, her long dark hair spilling over her shoulders. She's looking up and around, like she's looking for something.

My hand is on the door handle. I want to jump out of the car and go get her, but I can't. The path isn't clear. It may be three in the morning, but there's a wrought iron gate, security system, alarm—I wouldn't be able to get to her fast enough, even if I went in with guns blazing.

Before I can think of a plan to get her attention, a stocky man with a head of dark hair comes out and takes her by the shoulders, leading her back in. I don't have much in the way of equipment, but any idiot knows to bring binoculars.

What confuses the hell out of me is that when I get a good look at her face, she's smiling. Not her taunting, "fuck you" smile, but something softer. Childlike, almost. The man who came out to get her doesn't seem to be exerting any force, he's just guiding her.

What the fuck?

As the door closes, I have the sinking feeling it closes on the last opportunity I'm going to have to get Annabelle out before her whole world goes down in flames, and, if I can't find some way to get to her, her with it.

CHAPTER SEVENTEEN
Annabelle

It's gotten easy to pocket the pills.

Every morning my mom brings me one, a soft, stricken look on her face. She pets my hair and looks really sad, but never makes an attempt to stop them.

I call her Mommy. I hug her, a clingy, toddler-esque hug.

They all think I've had a nervous breakdown. Maybe I would have, if they had any fucking say. Good thing I've always been a good bullshitter.

Well, not always.

I guess I should thank Paul for that one.

Anyway, she comes back in the evening before bed to give me another one. I do something like play with her hair or pet her cheek. The other day I pressed mine against hers. I like to mix it up.

They don't think I'm capable of being this pleasant in a sober state, of faking it on this level, and I'm thankful that they underestimate me. I'm thankful for my waspish nature.

This morning after she gives me my pill, I shove it into its hiding place under my tongue, back far enough that I can talk, and I play my hand.

"I want to get you a present."

My tone is soft. I try to keep as close to the mannerisms I really affected on the night they had me drugged up.

"A present?" she asks.

I nod. "For your anniversary."

I've ruled out the probability of sneaking out. I may be able to arrange it if I had help from someone on the outside, but even then, I'm not sure. I've wandered around the house, scoping out the security, and Pietro takes paranoia to a new level.

Though I guess someone as awful as he is... maybe he's right to worry about people wanting to kill him.

They've stopped asking about Liam.

My mom tried at first, hoping to pick back up where she left off. I'm actually thankful I got sick that first night, because I was loose enough that I probably would've *actually* told her about Liam if she could've kept me talking just a little longer.

But I just kept telling them about Thor, as if I actually believed Thor was my boyfriend. My knowledge of Thor being no more than what I picked up watching a single superhero movie, I eventually had to start making shit up.

They think I've lost my mind. It's all good. It's been fun, here and there.

But I'm ready to be done. No more fighting, no more faking, no more bullshit. Freedom, for the first time in my life.

I'll do anything to get it, even hug my mom and act like they finally broke my brain.

Pietro must be so pleased with himself.

"You don't have to get me anything, honey," she tells me.

"Having you home again is present enough."

"No," I say, but pleasantly, with a smile. "I want one I can wrap. I know what I want to get, but it's a surprise. It's at the mall. Could you have someone drive me there so I can buy it? I'll need a little money. I'll ask Paul for some when he gets home."

She offers a pained nod. "I'll take you to the mall. You sister can come, she'll help you pick something out."

"No, not her." I frown at this. "Maybe Greg could take me. I don't want you to see it, I want it to be a surprise when you open it at your party."

"I'll ask," she tells me.

I nod pleasantly and lie down with my head on my pillow. They've moved me back into my old bedroom, now that I'm able to function.

Mom pulls back the covers that I'm on top of and I wiggle until she frees them, then she places the blanket around me and tucks me in like I'm five years old. Leaning down, she gives me a kiss on each cheek and stands.

"Good night, Annabelle."

"Good night, Momma."

Greg gets the green light to take me to the mall.

He doesn't seem too thrilled about it, but I can't say I blame the guy.

Well, until he calls me a retard under his breath, then I want to punch him in the face.

I've maintained the guise long enough at this point though, I'm not worried that people are suspicious. I'm not as vigilant as I once was, and I don't think I need to be.

"I think something engraved," I tell him, gazing out the window. "Something silver. A picture frame."

"Sure," he says, giving zero fucks.

I gasp. "Oh no, I forgot to get money from Paul."

He rolls his eyes. "I've got your money."

The rest of the ride is pretty quiet. My wheels are turning as I watch out the window, debating what to do. I'd like to make a break for it if I get a chance, but I don't know how to go about it. Not the running part, that's pretty self-explanatory, but where will I go that they can't find me when I don't even have any money?

Today isn't about escaping, it's about taking note of everything I can, seeing what kind of leeway Greg gives me. The thought of having to go back there tonight is absolutely withering, but I'm also aware that if I escape, Liam won't know where I've gone and then I *definitely* won't see him ever again.

It's hardly a deciding factor though. A bummer, yes, but I don't trust my mother or Pietro and I don't know how long I'll be able to keep up the pretense of being drugged stupid.

My plan at the moment is to figure it out as I go.

That's the plan.

Until I'm walking through the mall toward the store where I'm supposed to pick a gift, and I spot Liam in the middle of the corridor, letting some young guy chat his ear off about switching cell phone providers.

My stomach sinks. My heart leaps. I miss a step.

But he's here.

He's here.

I'm afraid I'm dreaming. I'm afraid I'm drugged up and I just don't know it. I'm afraid I'm at my mother's house with a needle in my vein and none of this is real.

My feet struggle to maintain a normal pace when all I want to do is bound over to him and leap into his arms.

I can't keep the grin off my face. Fortunately, it goes along with my happy-go-lucky little self, but every second that passes in such close proximity, but unable to speak to him, feels like an hour.

I walk into the store, heart slamming in my chest, and I try to act normal. I don't know what his plan is anyway, and I don't want to alarm Greg.

I can't concentrate on the task at hand. I wander around looking at gifts, trying not to look out the window, trying not to draw attention.

But *oh my God*.

He came for me.

I could literally skip with joy. Greg, not so much.

I've been in the store for ten minutes and he's already sighing impatiently at regular intervals.

"You 'bout ready?"

"Nope," I tell him, picking up a trinket box.

"I thought you said you wanted a frame. You looked at all the frames."

I give him a mildly disapproving look. "What's your rush, grumpy?"

"I gotta piss."

"So go," I say, bending to inspect yet another engraved box.

He doesn't, but I keep lingering, looking at every damn thing I can, and finally he walks over to the lady behind the bathroom.

Jerking a finger toward the employee area behind her, he asks, "You got a bathroom back there?"

She smiles and shakes her head apologetically. "No, sir. The nearest one is the food court, just four or five storefronts down."

He grumbles and makes his way over to me. "Are you done yet?"

"I'm not. Soon," I tell him, smiling. "I need to ask the lady about engraving. Why don't you just go pee so you're not in such a hurry."

I don't expect this to work. I expect to be locked down better, guarded, but he thinks my brain is a soft boiled egg and has no idea I'm wily.

"When I get back, we're buying something," he tells me in warning. "Make up your mind."

"I've got it narrowed down to three," I assure him.

It feels like a box of butterflies has been unleashed in my gut as he meanders out the door, and I wait, because I can't leave the store until I'm sure he's not within range to see me.

I don't have to.

Liam comes into the store and I can't even stop myself—I run at him, throwing my arms around his neck. He grabs me, fisting a hand in my hair, not roughly, and lifts me against him.

"I thought I'd never see you again," he says, burying his face in my neck.

I could actually die of happiness right now. "You came."

He nods, pulling back to look me in the eye. "I came."

I literally feel tears burning in my eyes, but my gaze jumps to the window. "We have to go. Now. He won't be gone long."

I lace my fingers through his and go to drag him out of the store, ready to run, but he doesn't move.

"Wait."

I turn back, eyes wide. "We need every second we can get. Where did you park?"

"There are things you need to know about me," he says, meeting my gaze. "And one thing I need to know before we run."

"What?" I ask, impatient, unable to believe he's wasting time like this.

"Will they cancel the party if you go missing?"

With three days before the big event? "I doubt it. It's too late now."

He nods slowly, then squeezes my hand and takes the lead, pulling me along.

"Why?" I ask, confused.

"I can't say here, too many people." Then, glancing back at me over his shoulder, he asks, "Do you have any idea what I do for a living?"

Hesitantly, I say, "I have a few guesses."

"Are any of them something you can't live with?"

I glance at the people we're moving past. He's taller, so he has longer legs and is moving much faster, but I'm jogging to keep up.

I'm not positive what he's getting at, but I sure have an idea. Everything Paul and my mother have implied about him circles my mind, but even with the evidence, it's a hard thing to believe.

But it doesn't matter.

"No," I tell him.

"Are you sure?" he asks, still moving.

We've made it to an exit so he pushes open the door and we hustle out to the parking lot.

"We're outside now, can't you just tell me?" I say, since I'd prefer we speak plainly.

He yanks me up against him and my breath catches, my

hands moving to his hard, muscled chest. My eyes melt with desire at the exact moment he states, "I'm a contract killer. I kill people for money. Good people, bad people, doesn't make a difference. I'm supposed to kill you. I'm not going to. This is my car."

He lets go of me and I stumble, my jaw slack as he opens the passenger door and heads around to the driver's side, sparing me a glance once he gets there.

I haven't moved. A lot to process in the space of a few seconds. I force my feet into motion, heart hammering, and fall into the passenger seat, yanking the door shut. I feel vaguely sick, but I don't want him to see it and think… I'm not even sure.

He stabs the key into the ignition and fires up the engine. "Still want to go with me?" he asks one more time.

"Yes," I say softly, though not without trepidation.

We're on the road for a few minutes before I find my words. He's preoccupied anyway, checking mirrors and changing lanes.

Greg will have made it back to the store by now. If he isn't already, Pietro will be looking for me.

The first question I ask isn't the one I was expecting to fall out of my mouth after such an admission.

"Where are you taking me?"

He glances over at me and looks a little unsure. "I have a cabin a couple hours away. It's remote so it'll be a good place for you to lay low."

"Are you staying there with me?"

He's quiet for a full minute. Finally he shakes his head no. "I can't. I'll come check on you as much as I can, but… I have some things to take care of first."

I nod, thinking of what he said earlier. I don't know what to ask. I don't know what I'm allowed to ask.

"Who hired you to kill me?"

Liam sighs. It's drawn out and tired, and I almost feel bad for asking, but then I don't, because... well, it seems like the kind of thing I should know.

"It wasn't specifically to kill you. I can't give you all the details right now. I don't want you to worry about it."

But I want to know. I really want to know. I want to know what job he is going to finish up, because if one of his 'jobs' was killing me, it's not too hard to guess what that other one might entail.

"Who are you going to kill?" I ask quietly.

His gaze moves to mine wordlessly, and I can see the skepticism on his face. Normally he hides his thoughts, his feelings, so I'm not sure if it's intentional or not, but I have a feeling it's important either way.

He doesn't answer me. His gaze returns to the road, and he checks mirrors a few times.

I accept that he won't answer that one for now, but I have another one I can't get out of my head.

"Can I ask you something else?"

"Yes." He's terse. It makes me nervous.

"When... when did you decide not to kill me?"

His silence stretches on for what feels like forever. My cheeks flush and I jump to conclusions like it's an Olympic sport and I'm going for the gold.

Swallowing, I try again. "Did you decide before you kissed me?"

I think he isn't going to answer me for another long moment, but then he finally utters a low, "No."

That's... not comforting.

I look out at the road ahead of me, thinking of where my

head was then.

I trusted him already. I followed him out of my guarded house into a secluded, wooded area.

And he still planned to kill me.

Paul's venomous words about how easy I was echo in my head and I hug myself protectively.

"I'm sorry," he finally says. "I'm sure that's not what you wanted to hear."

I shake my head very slightly, but don't look at him. "I wanted the truth. How were you planning to do it?"

He looks over at me again, and he still hasn't gone back to his usual stoicism. I guess that's a good sign.

"That's why you wouldn't have sex with me," I realize, right then. Dull horror and abject humiliation wash over me and I can't look at him.

Oh, my God. He must think I'm the biggest idiot in the world.

And for all the lost days I have and my trouble with timelines, *that* night I remember vividly. I know how I felt, how I thought maybe he felt. It's not foggy or unclear. I was sure I was safe with him.

In the company of a man who still, in the moment he was kissing me and touching my naked body, planned to murder me.

I'm quiet for a long, long time.

He lets me stew and doesn't bother me, but he keeps driving and doesn't ask again if I want to reconsider. I'm not sure if it's a good thing or a bad thing, but I'm thankful for it, because I'm having a really hard time processing what he just revealed.

It's a little longer before I start to wonder what *he's* feeling, sitting there quietly after spilling difficult secrets, waiting on my judgment.

I reach over tentatively and rest a hand on his thigh. His gaze jerks to mine, wary and untrusting, and I offer a little smile.

"I'm glad you changed your mind."

I expect—hope for—some relief on his face, but none appears. His features are still taut with tension, and he doesn't look at me as he says, "I'm not a good person, Annabelle. Maybe you thought I was because of everything with Paul, but I'm not."

Even after what he just told me, I'm not so sure about that.

Remembering his interference with Paul is also a little confusing—why put any effort whatsoever into keeping Paul from hurting me if he planned to turn around and kill me himself? Wouldn't Paul have just saved him some time if he killed me instead? Maybe he didn't get paid if Paul did it. I guess that would make sense.

I want to ask, but I also don't. I just want to drop this whole ugly topic.

The fact of the matter is, Liam is all I've got now. He's a much better hand than Paul, and I don't want to question him. It's sad that all of my hands have wanted to kill me at one point in time, but maybe I'm more vexing than I realized.

I laugh a little at that, but the laugh verges on hysterical.

Liam looks over at me cautiously, and I smile. "It's okay." I pause, realizing I mean it, and then I repeat, "It's okay."

"What I do…?"

I nod, still touching him. This isn't how I envisioned our reunion going in my fantasies, but to hell with it. I went all in when I ran with him, and there's no point picking things apart.

"It's okay," I say again.

I try not to think about what I'm telling him I'm okay with. I try not to wonder exactly who he's going to kill, or picture how it might happen.

I try to convince myself I feel cold all over because of the weather, despite my rosy cheeks and the toasty heat blowing out of the vents in his dashboard.

I can't consider the possibility that I'm making a deadly mistake.

CHAPTER EIGHTEEN
Liam

She hates me.

She's afraid of me.

I'm not sure exactly which is true, but one of them must be.

This is why I didn't want to tell her. Normal people aren't okay with shit like this. She isn't like me and Raj was right; she isn't cold enough.

Her hand is still on my thigh, but I think she just hasn't figured out how to move it.

I feel… uncomfortable. Like it matters more than it should that she's judging me, and at the same time fucking idiotic for even imagining it might go any other way.

You can't just tell a girl who's romanticized you that when she was kissing you and begging you to fuck her, you planned to kill her. You just can't do that. And if you do, you can't expect her to still be psyched about you.

I knew that.

I knew better than to tell her, but I didn't want to trap her, either. I assumed she had some fairy tale about me concocted in her mind, and I needed her to know how far off she was so she didn't feel tricked when she inevitably figured it out.

I just wanted to be wrong. I just wanted her to accept the rotten parts of me and still look at me like her fucking savior. I feel stupid thinking that was a possibility, and even dumber for wanting it in the first place.

God, what a fucking sap.

It's a long ride to the cabin. Annabelle doesn't say much and I never do. Knowing it's a long walk once we get there, I stop off at the last gas station before my exit.

"Last stop," I tell her, pushing open the car door and climbing out.

She climbs out, stretching her arms above her head and looking at the grimy little gas station.

I don't say a word to her, just head inside.

It doesn't feel like she's gonna stay, and I guess I don't blame her.

I'll let her get some sleep tonight, and then tomorrow when I bring her some more supplies, we can talk about her exit plan. Me, I'm not sticking around here after the job, but I'll help her out, and she can stay at my cabin as long as she needs to.

I know there's no meat at the cabin, so while she pees I grab a few sticks of jerky and a couple of candy bars to take to the register. My eye catches on a basket of fresh fruit on the counter. I grab a couple of apples in one hand, putting them down as I pull out my wallet with the other.

I go ahead and buy gas, too, since I have to drive back to the damn city tonight.

Back at the car, I drop the bag in the floor next to Annabelle's legs. She spots an apple and pulls it out of the bag, smiling faintly as she drags her nails across a dimple in the skin.

"Who knew apples caused so much trouble," she said lightly.

"I think God, or the serpent, or… some combination of biblical characters," I return, starting the car back up.

She smiles faintly but doesn't respond.

A short time later, I pull off the dusty road we've been traveling and roll to a stop in front of the barred metal gate. As I put the car in park, I notice Annabelle cutting glances at me out of the corner of my eye.

"We're here," I say, reaching over and grabbing the bag from the gas station.

"Okay," she says, not sounding terribly confident.

I guess looking at it from her perspective, the guy who just told her he'd been contracted to murder her drove her out into the middle of nowhere and is now telling her to follow him into a wooded area with no cottage in sight.

"How far is it?" she asks as she closes her passenger door.

"About a half hour, maybe 40 minutes if you're slow."

That's what I told her, because that was the truth in my experience.

Over an hour later when we still weren't there, I learned Annabelle was not the outdoorsy type.

Stumbling over a branch that was camouflaged by wet leaves, Annabelle catches herself on the soggy ground and blows out a breath of frustration as she pushes herself back up. "Is it much farther?" she grinds out.

Cracking a smile, I glance back at her. She's frazzled and cold and sweaty at the same time. Her pale cheeks are flushed and she looks so damn cute, I kinda wish she didn't hate me so I could give her a kiss.

Shaking my head, I continue on. "Should only be a few more minutes."

Luckily the path is a little clearer here, and we make it to the cabin about 15 minutes later.

It's a simple cottage—ramshackle wood construction with a stone chimney. There's no heat to the thing, so it's only warmed by the fireplace and lit by the candles and oil lantern. It has windows, but they're cloudy and the whole place is obviously dark, since I haven't been here. There's a small clearing in front of the house and a little creek with a crude footbridge.

I steal a glance at her and she looks nervous. When she notices me looking, her expression clears and she takes a few steps, heading over the footbridge ahead of me.

"We made it," she says brightly.

I wonder what she thinks about it. The house she grew up in was obviously nice and big, but then Paul bought them that little box. Still, it was probably twice the size of this cottage.

"It's gonna be chilly," I warn her, catching up and drawing the keys out of my pocket, working the cottage key off my key ring. There's not much point in a lock clear out here, but I have one anyway. Can't be too careful when it comes to being prepared for the unexpected. Suppose someone did find me out here—at least I'd have another minute to react.

"I'll leave this here with you. It's the only key, so you'll have to let me in when I come back."

She nods her head, hugging herself as we walk through the door.

"You probably shouldn't wander too far from the cottage though. Doesn't seem like you're..."

I don't want to say she's completely incapable of surviving in the wilderness, but she's already nodding, because she's discovered the same thing about herself in the last hour and a half.

"I won't."

It's pretty dark at this point, so she waits by the door while I find the lantern. Once it's lit, I pull a full box of candles out of one of the cupboards and drop it on the short stretch of counter.

Annabelle comes inside slowly, checking it out. It's still pretty dark in the corners, but she can see to get around. It's not much. A red flannel-print couch with a rough wood end table and lantern next to it. A table with a single chair, for eating alone. The kitchen isn't much of a kitchen without power—some cupboards with pots and dishes, a couple of drawers, some utensils, some matches and flashlights and tools. Beside the counter is a case of bottled water and a box full of toilet paper.

She opens the cupboards one by one, and finally finds some food in the third one. Not a ton of food, but some granola bars, a half-eaten jar of peanut butter, a bag of flour, saltine crackers, half a dozen cans of tomato soup.

"I'll bring you some bread tomorrow," I tell her.

She nods, lips pressed together in what I can only call a brave face.

"And whatever else you need," I add.

She manages a smile. "Thank you. It'll be fine. There's... no stove?"

I nod and reach into a lower cupboard, pulling out the pot I hang over the fireplace. I nod to the cold, dark fireplace while holding the pot until she gets the picture.

"Oh. Okay. Cool."

"It's just for a few days," I tell her.

She nods, but still looks anxious.

I grab a book of word search puzzles off the countertop and hand it to her.

She regards me with raised eyebrows.

"Not a whole lot to do out here," I explain. "There's a pond not too far behind the cottage, but... it's not really fishing weather, and I'm gonna go ahead and guess you're not the outdoorsy type anyway."

Full-on grinning, she asks, "What gave me away?"

I merely shake my head and make my way to the fireplace so I can get the place to start warming up.

Annabelle wanders around a little more, then takes a seat at the edge of the couch and watches me work. "Do you come out here a lot?"

"Not a lot."

"How long can you stay tonight?"

I have to pull the night shift guarding the junkyard, but I can stay for a few hours. After the tense car ride, I wasn't so sure she'd really want me to.

"I've got a bit," I say.

"We should've grabbed food on the way," she realizes.

I smile, but my back's to her so she can't see me. "I'll bring food tomorrow night."

"Is that the next time I'll see you?"

My shoulders tense at the question. I don't know how tomorrow's gonna go. It could be pretty bad, if the worst case scenario plays out. I don't know exactly how Raj gets all of his information and I don't know how Pietro will react to what I've done today. Could be I won't be able to come back tomorrow, because I'll have a shitstorm to deal with.

"I'm not sure. That's the soonest. I'll have to go back to my apartment in the morning and wait to see what happens after today. Assuming all goes smoothly, I'll come back tomorrow evening."

Now she looks anxious again. "How will I know if things don't go... smoothly? If you just don't show up, I won't know how to... I won't know anything. How long do I wait?"

Standing from my crouched position, I abandon the fire and head into the bedroom to get into my lockbox. I don't expect her to follow me, but by the time I'm turning to go back to the living area, she's there in the doorway.

She glances at the cell phone I offer to her. "It's a burner." I hand her another small, cylindrical object. "This is good for about a dozen charges. This phone'll be yours in case you need to reach me. Obviously you should only make contact sparingly, if at all, but if something goes wrong or you need me for something, I'll put my number in it for you and you'll have a way."

"Thanks," she says, taking both items, regarding them awkwardly. She glances around for somewhere to put them, but it's pretty sparse. She settles on shoving them in the puffy front pocket of her sweatshirt.

I'm not the most socially graceful in the best of situations, and this is definitely not that. Annabelle stays just inside the bedroom door, and I turn to squeeze past her.

"Wait," she says, a hand tentatively grazing my side. Even through my clothes, her touch makes me tense.

I watch her with a straight face, but I almost feel bad because she's completely open, and she looks more than a little unsure of herself as her fingers trail across my hip. There's not much sound out here, just the faint hum of the creatures outside, so I can hear her gulp.

Stilling her much smaller hand with mine, I stop her, brushing her off. "You don't have to do that."

Falling back a little, almost shrinking, she says, "You don't want me to?"

"You've had a lot to process since I took you from the mall. I don't expect you to feel the same way now you did before. You don't owe me anything; I saved you because I wanted to."

Scowling, she says, "*Owe* you anything?"

I nod once, gruff. I don't like this conversation and I'd just as soon go show her the rest of the shit she needs to know so I can leave.

"Liam..." She looks down at the creaky floor beneath us, scuffing her toe awkwardly, then back up at me, this time with a little smile and a roll of her eyes. "I still *want* you. I'm still *grateful* to you. You're still very much my Thor."

"Huh?"

Shaking her head dismissively, she said, "Doesn't matter. Did I *expect* that you were originally supposed to off me? Well, no. But what are you gonna do? Plus, I'm used to it; I've literally never been fucked by someone who *didn't* want to kill me at one point in time."

Grabbing her around the waist with one arm, I yank her up against me. Excitement jumps in her eyes and she braces her hands on my chest, biting down on her lower lip.

"I didn't *want* to, it was just a job," I correct her.

She doesn't seem to care as her eyes follow my mouth.

I'm still a little bothered though. "Paul was your first?"

"Paul is shit and we don't have to talk about Paul," she says, echoing my earlier words. Then, with relish, she adds, "Ever. Again."

I have to smile. I like this Annabelle. Not Paul's Annabelle, the robotic, miserable one, but the unbroken, full-of-surprises Annabelle.

My Annabelle.

Holding my gaze, she says, "This doesn't change anything between us, not for me."

"You still want me?" I murmur, dipping my head to trail a few kisses along her jaw.

Fisting her hands in my shirt, she says, "Oh, yes." Then, a little less breathy, she teases, "You still want *me*?"

In response, I drop my hands to her ass and lift her up. Her legs wind naturally around my waist and I haul her over to the bed, prepared to show her just what a stupid question that was.

CHAPTER NINETEEN
Annabelle

The breath whooshes out of me as Liam drops me onto the bed—not so much from the force of the fall, but the sight of him yanking his shirt over his head already.

Oh my God, finally.

I can't rip my eyes from the hard, muscled planes of his body. I've never seen anything like it in real life. I want to drag my tongue along the ridges just to feel proof of what my eyes are telling me.

I'm pretty sure I'm out of my league here, but I give him a sultry little smile like I'm totally not.

"I like the look of you on my bed," he tells me, taking a step closer before he starts unbuckling his pants.

My heart soars. I might die of happiness and lust and a general overdose of positive feelings.

"You know what I'd like even better?" he asks.

"I can think of so many things," I say, watching his pants hit the floor and gulping again.

He smiles, and my heart does a somersault. I wish I could think of something clever to say to make him do it again.

"Less clothing," he states, quirking an eyebrow at all the

clothes I still have on.

Without bravado, I state, "I think I've forgotten how to use my hands."

He grins again, and I'm very pleased with myself. Then he bends, bracing his hands on the bed, and suddenly he's hovering over me, and my amusement dies, quickly replaced by a yearning I've never felt before.

"I can help with that," he tells me, bracing his weight on one hand and using the other to grab my shirt. It's a sweatshirt so I'm not totally sure what he's planning to do—unbutton it?—until he suddenly fists it, lifting it, until I'm arching off the bed, closer to him. He holds me like that, sort of suspended, and as his lips brush the sensitive nerve endings around my mouth, the throbbing starts. I squeeze my legs together and he feels me. His eyes move to mine, dark and tense and passionate, and as much as Paul tried to possess me, he never could, not like this. I'm wholly Liam's right now.

He releases his hold on my shirt and drops me on the bed. I huff another breath out and go to lift my shirt (my hands have suddenly remembered how to function, because I *need* to feel his skin against mine) but his hands are on mine, pulling them away. His hands move up under my shirt, teasing the cool skin of my belly. Goosebumps rise up all over, and the chills are a stark contrast to the heat between us.

Finally, he pulls my shirt up. I twist and turn to make it easier, and a few seconds later he's flung my shirt somewhere behind us, the thump of the phone reminding me that maybe we shouldn't have thrown it.

He doesn't seem to care. His eyes rake over my terribly unsexy bra like it's made of the most revealing lace, and then he's reaching behind me to unclasp it.

I'm held against him as he does this, and I can't help kissing his skin. My lips move across the giant pec in my face until I reach the nipple. My tongue shoots out and circles it, sucking it lightly, and he rewards me with a groan.

I can't shake the feeling that time is running out. I want to do everything with him, learn every inch of his body, try everything I've always wondered about, and it doesn't feel like we have enough time.

I have no idea how much time we have.

The thought is sobering, but my bra joins my shirt on the floor and the sudden heat of his hands on my breasts pulls me right back into the heat of the moment.

"What do you like?" he asks, massaging my breasts, but meeting my gaze.

My heart races so hard in my chest, he has to feel it. "I... uh, I'm not sure."

He nods once, considering, then he releases my breasts and grabs my arms, jerking them above my head.

I gasp, squirm, and then he's between my legs, wearing nothing but briefs. His hardness pushes against me, ready to invade, and oh, God, how I want him to.

He holds my hands down pretty hard, but not hard enough to bruise. This isn't like what I've experienced before, and I assure him of that when he asks, "This?"

"Yes." I'm breathing so hard, you'd think he's already fucking me. If he doesn't soon, he may need to build one of those footbridges over this bed.

He thrusts his hips against me, holding my gaze, and I gasp again, trying to twist, but he still has my arms above my head. He tightens his grip when I try to move, and leans in to kiss my neck as his free hand starts at my breasts and trails lightly down my body.

"Oh, God," I murmur, twisting again as his finger circles my belly button. I know where he's heading and I just want him to *get there*, but he knows that, so he takes a detour, over to my hips and down my thigh.

"Tell me you want me," he says.

"I want you," I tell him.

"What do you want?"

"Touch me."

He smiles, inching closer, but just working back up and down my thigh. "Is that how you ask?"

I pull at my hands again, but he doesn't let them go. "Please," I add. "Please touch me. I want you to touch me."

I don't know what combo of words he's looking for, but I'll write them all down for him later if he'll just fucking put his fingers where I want them.

Finally those goddamn beautiful fingers move inward, skating across my entrance so lightly that I have to whimper.

"Liam," I murmur, rotating my hips.

"I wish we had longer," he says, echoing my own feelings.

Logically, I want to know how long we do have, but there's no place for logic in my mind right now.

I arch up toward him, unable to use my hands, but wanting him to kiss me.

Taking my hint, he leans down like he's going to kiss me, but instead hovers above my mouth. My eyes are closed, and as I open them to see why he's stopped, he thrusts a finger inside me. I gasp, and he catches it with his mouth, tongue thrusting as his fingers explore.

"Oh," I try to murmur, pleasure swirling inside of me with his every movement. I try to kiss him back but I'm already lost, and he moves a second finger inside of me, thrusting deep. "Oh, God."

I pull on my arms again and he frees me that time, so I can hold onto him. I ride his hand, eyes closed. I can't focus on kissing and my head falls back, so he kisses his way down my chest. He sucks on my nipple as his thumb circles my clit and I cry out.

Then I want to *actually* cry as his fingers leave me.

I make a faint sound of protest, brow furrowing with disapproval, until I see his head moving down my body.

"Oh, God," I say, fisting my hands in the bed sheets.

He looks up at me, giving me a wicked smile that jumpstarts my heart on its own, then his breath is on me, and his fingers are spreading me, and I'm already bursting with need when his tongue pushes inside me.

I cry out again, sagging back against the bed, and his tongue makes quick work of finding the spot his thumb left wanting.

I'm panting like an animal as his beautiful mouth works magic between my legs. I gasp, startled, when it feels like he sucks it, then his tongue is circling, hitting just the right spots, and I can't breathe. He's bringing my body to a fever pitch; I'm afraid to breathe, afraid to do anything that might stop this building pleasure from completely consuming me.

He locks on, like he knows I'm close, the prodding from his tongue a little harder, a little more deliberate, and I can feel faint discomfort from my nails biting into my palms, but someone could shoot me and I wouldn't be able to feel less…

And then I feel more, so much more. Pleasure shoots through me like lightning, rippling and zapping all the strength from my limbs.

Spent, I fall back against the bed. Liam comes up and I wrap my arms around him, pulling him against me. His weight's a little crushing, but I don't care. Who needs to breathe when you're basking in the glow of a great orgasm?

Turns out me, after a couple minutes. He rolls over on his side and watches me.

"That was lovely," I inform him.

"It was." He misses a beat. "Ready?"

"For?"

He grins, and I'm a little tired and boneless still, but a rush of tenderness washes over me as he hovers over me again. His hardness presses against my thigh and my greedy lady bits tingle. I drop my hand between us, pushing my hand down the front of his boxer briefs and take him in my hand.

"I don't care if it's your 50th orgasm, we're not done here until I've been inside you," he states.

"Oh, I concur. I don't think I can survive 50, but I'm ready to go for 2."

I love watching pleasure play out on his features as my hand moves up and down his length, pulling, squeezing, experimenting with different pressures. I don't know what feels good to him, and I want time to learn.

"Do you know how badly I wanted to fuck you that night against the tree?" he asks.

Just hearing the words from those beautiful lips excites me.

"Well, you can fuck me now. Hard, fast, slow—anyway you want me."

He groans, burying his face in my neck and dislodging my hand.

I scoot up on my elbows, waiting for direction. He peels off his underwear and tosses them to the clothing graveyard, and I'm suddenly so *excited* that this man is about to be *mine*.

Possessive. Never felt that before.

Liam.

Mine.

I like it.

He grabs my hips, lifting me. I follow his lead and get on my hands and knees on the bed. Heart pounding, I brace one hand on the bed and one hand on the headboard.

Liam comes up behind me, grabbing my hips and repositioning them. I love the way he handles my body. It's like he knows just what I like somehow. It's like his body knows mine already.

His hand moves over the curve of my ass, then settles between my legs. He pushes a finger inside me again, then two, thrusting a few times.

I moan, moving against his hand.

He stops again, anchoring one hand on my hip and using the other to guide himself to my entrance. Anticipation is a brutal bitch as he butts just the head against me.

"Ready?"

"Fuck yes," I tell him.

A low rumbly laughter that I don't even take time to appreciate, because then he plows inside me.

"Oh, God, yes," I say breathlessly. He pulls back and pushes in again, slowly, testing my response. Satisfied that I'm apparently all good, he then starts bucking into me harder. He picks up the pace with each thrust until he's pounding me so hard that I can't push hard enough against the headboard, and as he fucks the hell out of me, balls slapping, driving so deep inside me that I don't know how he'll ever find his way out, I'm also inching closer and closer to hitting my head.

"Fuck," I say, giving up my hold on the bed. My boobs are crushed against the pillow, but pushing with the second hand keeps me from getting a concussion.

Liam doesn't stop. My muscles ache with the effort of pushing away from the headboard, but he's pounding some magical spot and it's all I can concentrate on.

"Liam," I cry out senselessly, just needing to make noise.

He angles his hips just slightly, and all of a sudden I can't breathe again. The friction is too much. I feel like I'm going to lose my mind. I'm so close, so close, I can't think or speak or breathe.

And then pleasure erupts within me, but it's not like before—it's better. I'm a mindless, pleasure-seeking animal as I slither down the bed, pushing back against him with every last ounce of strength in my body. Oh, my god.

Liam groans, thrusting deep. I know he's coming so I try to move with him, clenching him and moving until he's ridden out his own orgasm.

Then I collapse.

I almost can't believe we both survived that.

I'm exhausted and sweaty, and oh my God, what a wonderful appendage.

"Holy fucking hell," I murmur against the sheets.

Liam snorts, pulling my limp body over against him.

I fling an arm across his torso and snuggle up, more satisfied and content than I've ever been in my life.

I'm never letting this man go.

Never.

CHAPTER TWENTY
Annabelle

"Annabelle."

My eyes flutter open and I lift my arm above my head to stretch, knocking Liam in the jaw.

"Oh, God!" I immediately drop my arm, looking at him, worried. "I'm sorry. Are you okay?"

Rubbing his jaw with a faint smirk on his face, he tells me, "I've had worse."

I'm still a little lazy from sleep, but just looking at him makes me all happy. That post-orgasm fondness doesn't seem to have dissipated yet. I want to curl up with him and kiss his beautiful, chiseled face.

"I can see that you're comfy, but you need to get up. I have to get going, and I still have to show you a few things."

My face promptly falls.

Somehow, in the rush of my newly won freedom, the glow of our passionate sexy time, and my sudden, all-consuming fondness for this man….

Well, I forgot he had to leave.

"No, not yet," I balk, my gaze jumping to the window. My

stomach sinks when I see it's dark outside. "Why'd you let me sleep?"

"It's been a long day," he tells me.

Only then do I realize he's completely dressed, and his skin is cool and a little red like he's been outside.

"I can sleep when you leave—literally all I have to do is sleep."

There's no point arguing about it, so he doesn't, even though I want to, like that will rewind time and give me those precious hours back that I completely wasted.

Liam pats the stack of my discarded clothing he's folded and left on his side of the bed. "Get dressed."

I pout, but drag my lazy ass out of bed and grudgingly pull my clothes on.

It feels like he's going to be gone forever. And I'm going to be alone out here in some remote forest. And it took like three hours to get here, so even when he's on his way back to me, it's going to take a long time.

Goddammit.

I want this job to be over so he doesn't have to leave me anymore. Then we can….

I freeze, one leg in my jeans.

Then we can what?

I don't know what happens when the job ends. I have no idea.

This is why I need more time! I need answers to questions like these. Do I have more time? Do *we* have more time? His words from earlier come back to me and I don't know what they mean. He wants more time with me, in general, because it's nearly over? Or he just wanted more time before he had to leave for work?

Oh, God.

What if I just found him and I'm about to lose him already?

I don't know what kind of life he has when he isn't doing this. I don't know what he has to go back to.

I don't know if he ever planned on taking me.

He was already going against orders to save me, but what if it was just that? He couldn't stomach killing me, so he didn't, but now we go our separate ways? I don't want separate ways. I want more time.

The cabin feels smaller, colder than it did before. I'm scared, and it embarrasses me to admit that, even if only to myself.

His back is to me. I clear my throat to get his attention, and he glances at me over his shoulder.

"You have to leave right now?"

"In a few minutes," he tells me.

Dread. A steady stream of it, seeping through every part of my body.

"What are you going back to?"

Liam doesn't say anything for a minute, and that scares me even more. Finally he moves, stepping forward and opening what I guess is a closet. He kneels down, prying up the floor boards inside.

"What are you doing?" I ask tentatively.

He brings a black duffel bag up out of the floorboard and holds it up for me to see. "This is a go bag. You know what that is?"

I shake my head no.

"In case everything goes to shit and you need to get the hell out of here, take this. There's cash, supplies, a phone, and a phone number in it. Remember I told you I don't trust many people?"

I nod as he unzips the bag and holds up a folded piece of

paper.

"I trust him. Anything happens to me and I don't come back for you, you take this and you run."

"I run?" My mind is racing, trying to process everything. "Run where? If *what* happens to you? Why wouldn't you come back for me? I'll never find my way out of these woods. If you don't come back for me, I'll die here."

Liam stands, walking over to me and placing a steadying hand on each shoulder. "Listen, I understand this is scary shit and I'm sorry I can't hold your hand through it right now, but I can't. I have to leave. And I have to leave here knowing that if anything happens to me, you know what to do."

I shake my head in denial, but he ignores me.

"If anything happens and I don't come back, call this number. Tell him what happened and who you are. He might not believe you. This isn't really my style. In that case, tell him…" He pauses, thinking. "Ask him how the ladies like the scar I gave him," he decides with a faint smile.

"That sounds like a good story. See, *or* you could scrap this whole work thing and stay here and tell me the story." Nodding enthusiastically, I say, "I vote that."

Tenderly caressing my jaw with his thumb, he tells me, "When I come back for you I'll tell you the story."

But what if you don't? It's right on the tip of my tongue, but I'm terrified speaking the words will invite the possibility into the universe.

"Please don't go," I say instead.

He drops his hand and I miss the contact instantly.

Turning away from me, he retrieves the bag. "There's a compass in here. You can keep heading east and you'll make it out of the woods eventually. If you have to call Ryder, tell him that I want you to have the sunset house and you need him to help you get there. Whatever's left that's mine, you can have. There's a go-bag there, too, under the floor in a closet, but you shouldn't need one. It's safe and secure and really nice there. It's on the beach. You'll like it."

"Don't talk about it like I'm going there. I don't want to go to any beach house unless you're going with me."

He ignores me again. "I have an account, a bank account. Ryder's on it. Tell him to give half to you."

I don't want to listen to anymore of this.

"Why do you have to go back?" I demand. "Who cares if you don't? Let's go to the beach house now. We can tell each other all the stories we want and have sex and eat food that isn't canned, or is canned, I don't care. Just *don't go*. If there's even a chance I'd have to use a go-bag and run away without you, it isn't worth it. Stay with me."

"I can't. I have to finish this."

"Says who?"

He shakes his head, remorseful but resolved. "Now that I've done this, saved you like this, crossed your family... I need to do this now more than ever."

"What are you *doing*?"

I feel dread just asking, like I don't really want the answer. But more than that I want to be armed with the same information he has, so I can talk him out of his own thought process.

"I won't tell you that. You'll figure it out after, but... You're not going to change my mind and I don't want you to look at me differently, so let's just leave it at that."

"I won't."

"Just... Annabelle, I have to leave. I don't have time to argue with you."

"I know you're going to kill someone," I continue. "Just tell me who. Is it Pietro? It has to be Pietro, right? You were afraid I was going to report back to him."

Instead of answering, he kisses me. I expect it to be a short, just to shut me up kind of kiss, but he lingers, and I'm already scared, so that scares me more. I hold onto him as he deepens the kiss, moan as he backs me up against the wall, and take him eagerly, greedily when he drops his jeans and pushes inside me.

I want to fight or fuck or do whatever it takes to keep him from leaving.

But it doesn't.

After he finishes, he remains inside me, pressed against the wall for a couple of minutes with his head on my shoulder. I hold on tight, full of terror and frustration and something that feels alarmingly like love. I'll call it fondness, that makes more sense. Fondness. Yeah.

Then he pulls out, and pulls back, and I can tell by the set of his features and his shoulders there's no point fighting. He's prepared for me to fight, his face a stoic mask, like he doesn't care, but I don't believe that anymore.

I don't fight. I'm seasoned at hedging my bets, and I know I won't win this one. I don't want to stress him out even more, so I follow him out the door to the little footbridge over the creek. There's a well of sadness inside me, and I'm pretty sure it's going to burst open the moment he leaves.

But God, how I *don't want* this to be the moment he leaves.

"There's wood for the fire inside. I brought some in while you were asleep. Keep it going if you can, it gets cold out here."

I *feel* cold, but it's not because of the weather.

"I've been alone for too much of my life," I tell him. "Don't make me be alone again."

"I promise I will do everything in my power to make sure you aren't," he tells me. "I'm a murderer, not a martyr; if I know I'm in too deep and I can't win, I *will* cut my losses and come back and we'll just run. I just don't want to do that. The loose ends need to be cleaned up. Then we don't have to run."

That does nothing to cheer me up, and I continue to look like he just ran over my favorite pet.

"And hey, if I don't come back, maybe you can tame Ryder," he tells me, lightly.

A thunderous scowl and a smack in the belly later, he is aware I don't find that funny.

"Nah, he's a dog anyway," he adds.

"I'm very stubborn, if you haven't noticed. I'm not interested in any other scoundrel. I only want you."

"I have noticed that," he said with a nod. "It's not always smart, you know."

I cross my arms stubbornly.

He smiles, a little smile. We're both too worried over what's waiting for him for either of us to exude much joy.

"Will you call me when your shift is over, before you go to sleep, just so I know everything's okay?" I ask him.

He hesitates, but eventually nods. "I'll try."

I don't really want an "I'll try" but I guess it will have to do. My formerly soaring heart is so heavy in my chest as he gives me one last kiss on the forehead and then makes his way across the foot bridge.

It's dark, so he disappears from my sight only a moment later.

The lump in my throat is big and real, and all I want to do is cry. I want to sit down on the forest floor and sob until I drop.

But it's cold, and he's coming back, so I don't want to get

sick. I head back into the cabin, lug one more heavy log over to throw on the fire, and sit down on the ugly plaid couch.

Despair creeps up over me, but it's not the same kind I'm used to. It feels so much less fair. A cloud of despair over an already miserable existence is one thing, but on the heels of such a high, of such all-consuming happiness?

It's unbearable.

I break down in sobs on the ugly plaid couch, and eventually cry myself to sleep.

Alone.

CHAPTER TWENTY ONE
Liam

Leaving her was a lot harder than I anticipated.

I didn't expect it to be hard at all. I knew what had to happen; I expected it to be *easier* now that she's safe and I'm free to go about my business, no longer distracted.

But I'm still distracted.

I'm also trying not to come off as paranoid. I shouldn't even know Annabelle has gone missing, and there's no guarantee Raj knows. I *hope* he doesn't, because if he does, that must mean they've canceled that party, and that's the last thing any of us wants. I've thought it over so much that cancelling the party seems almost crazy, but that's the outcome I want, so I'm not exactly unbiased.

I hate that I think about how she'll feel afterward, about my part in all this, about me. She says she's okay with it, but is she really? Would she be, if she realized the extent of it?

It has to be done though. Then Raj will have no reason to bother me and Annabelle won't have to fear her family. Realizing the way they'd been poisoning her with meds made me want to do this job even more. I have no remorse for what I'll help do to them.

I hear footsteps coming from inside the gate so I round the corner to see who it is. Lance. He has his gun and comes over to the other side of the gate, manning his post.

"Raj wants to see you."

I nod, abandoning my post but bringing the gun with me.

When I make it to his office, Raj has a map open, a smile on his face, a twinkle in his dark eyes. His mustache quirks up when he sees me, and I decide he hasn't heard about Annabelle.

"I need you tonight."

"Tonight?"

"Another opportunity has come up. Another boost."

I shift my weight, rubbing the back of my neck. "I still have an hour left before I can even go get some sleep. Are you sure you want to take that risk this close to the party?"

Nodding with enthusiasm, he says, "It'll be worth it."

"Another boost isn't included in my fee," I point out.

He smiles, unbothered. "Yes, yes. I'll make sure you get a bonus."

I don't like it. I'll steal if I have to, but I'm not a thief and this isn't my wheelhouse. I'm also uncomfortable with a change in the plan, knowing what I do about Annabelle. I've considered maybe no one will care that she's disappeared since she *is* an adult, but if she was lucid enough to run, or I 'stole' her out from under his nose, Pietro's pride won't be able to tolerate that.

Plus her stupid cow mother will play up her concern.

"Lance is here now, so you can go on home and get some sleep. Be back here at 7."

Given I was supposed to check on Annabelle tonight, this fucks everything up. Can't really say no, though. Don't want to raise any alarms this late in the game.

I'll just go to her now. I'm exhausted and didn't want to waste our time together sleeping, but I'll have to. Just a couple more days like this, then I'll be free to do as I please. With Annabelle.

I take Raj up on his offer to leave early. I swing by the store and grab Annabelle some bread, jelly, juice, a box of cereal, and a whole rotisserie chicken for good measure.

It's cold by the time I get there, of course.

Then I remember I left Annabelle my only key. Doesn't matter though, since apparently she didn't bother to lock the damn door.

I know there's very little chance the place was compromised, but I'm still uneasy as I walk through the cold cabin. She let the fire die, so I drop the food on the counter, grab a log and go over to get it going again. It doesn't look like she's eaten.

Anticipation moves through me as I head back to the bedroom, and there she is, bundled up in bed in the thick blankets.

It was worth the drive, I decide. Nearly falling asleep at the wheel and dragging myself through the forest. Climbing in bed next to her is all I wanna do, so I strip off my shirt, kick off my shoes, and do just that.

She stirs when I slide in next to her, then I wrap my cool arms around her warm body. It feels so good to have her in my arms.

Jumping, she turns to face me. Pleasure spreads all over her face when she sees me and causes my stomach to sink a little. Annabelle throws her arms around my neck and squeezes me.

"You came back."

"I told you I would," I tell her lightly, like it couldn't have gone any other way.

"What time is it?"

"Early. Go back to sleep."

"No, I don't wanna waste the time..."

"I've gotta get some sleep, too. I work again tonight."

Her mouth curves downward, but she curls up against my body, tucking her head under my chin, and in a couple minutes, Annabelle is asleep.

I wake up to the smell of something burning.

I jolt upward and jump out of bed, running out into the living room.

Annabelle is hunched over the pot over the fire, swearing at it. I don't do much to hide my amusement, and she glares at me over her shoulder.

"First it was too cold. It's not so easy to determine how hot it's getting over here."

I glance at the counter and see the bag of groceries has been unpacked. She carved the chicken and set out two plates. There's a glass of juice and a bowl beside each plate.

I go over to the fire and help her with the pot. It's hot and I don't want her to burn her hands or spill it everywhere.

I pour it into the bowls anyway, but the bottom of the pot is layered with scorched soup.

"How did you burn the soup?" I ask, shaking my head. She's

shifting anxiously and I don't want to make her feel worse, but damned if I can figure how this even happened.

"Your wood made the fire too hot," she accuses, even though that's illogical.

I wink at her. "Yeah, it did."

She narrows her eyes but smiles reluctantly. "Whatever. If it's not good, at least there's chicken."

"I'll eat every last bite," I assure her.

"Bet you wish you had that unimpressive deli sandwich now, don't you?" she jokes.

"I can get food later; I'm more concerned about feeding you. Especially if this is how your soup turns out," I add.

"There are, like, 40 granola bars in here; I think I'll survive." She stands on one side of the counter and I stand on the other since my table isn't equipped for two diners. "This chicken smells amazing," she tells me.

I take a drink of the room-temperature juice. "I didn't know what kind of cereal you liked. I figured Corn Pops are good without milk, so...."

"A very good choice, thank you. I'm a Cinnamon Toast Crunch kind of gal, but if there's no milk, Froot Loops. What's your favorite kind of cereal?"

I smile, eyes on my plate as I spear a piece of chicken. "That's what you wanna ask me? My favorite cereal?"

"I want to ask you everything, but I have to start somewhere," she reasons.

"Raisin Bran."

"Well, I can see straight into your soul now," she replies. After a second, she asks more seriously, "How long until you have to leave?"

I check my phone and make a face. "Couple hours. Maybe

three."

Annabelle sighs, but immediately brightens. "Well, we'll have to make the best of them then."

I nod in agreement. I don't want to think about tonight. Going back. No part of me wants to go, and I guess it must be because for the first time, there's a much better alternative waiting for me.

Annabelle pushes a piece of chicken into her mouth and watches me. After she swallows, she says, "You know, I don't even know your last name."

"Hunt," I supply.

"Liam Hunt?" Nodding approvingly, she says, "I like that."

Even though I'm still tired, I wish I hadn't slept so long. It's bound to be a long night, and I won't come back here afterwards. I decide it's best to warn her.

"I'll go back to my apartment in the city tonight after work. I'll sleep and then I'll have to go back to work, so I won't be back until tomorrow night. I should be able to spend the night with you here, but after I leave that time, I won't come back until the job is done. So if you need anything else, don't be shy, tell me and I'll bring it tomorrow."

Her face has darkened with disappointment but she nods, accepting it. Then, daring a glance up at me, she says, "Will you tell me what the job is now?"

I ignore the request, trying the soup. It isn't great, but still edible. "Not bad," I tell her.

Not letting me get away with it this time, she continues, "I take it that's a no? Why?"

I go over it one more time in my mind. Some of it I think she'd be okay with, but other parts... not so much. After it's done, it's done. But right now....

I can't risk her asking me not to do it. Because I'm going to. I'm going to finish the job, get the rest of my money, and then we can leave.

"You like warm weather?"

She gives me a dry look as she scoops up a spoonful of soup. "Slick subject change."

"Not a subject change. Just thinking about after the job is over."

That softens her a little, successfully changing the subject. "I was wondering about that. I wasn't sure what happens after. Do you have a life to go back to?"

"I don't, not exactly, but I want to build one. I told you about the sunset house. That's where I'm going. You can come with me, if you want to."

She can't help smiling. "I would like that. Is there a stove?"

That one makes me chuckle. "Yes, there's a stove. A whole kitchen, even."

"Fancy," she says, rubbing her hands together with relish.

I picture her there, bare toes in the sand with the waves lapping at the shore behind her, her pale skin darker from exposure to the sun.

Actually, I should probably pick up a sunscreen for her. Bet she burns easily.

"When?" she asks, bringing me out of my daydream.

"We'll leave in a few days. I booked you a plane ticket, figuring you might wanna come. Next week we'll be in another country, on a beach, with a new life."

Something she sorely needed, but I don't add that.

She seems really pleased. And she's forgotten to keep

bugging me about the job. Win-win.

CHAPTER TWENTY TWO
Annabelle

I nuzzle my face against Liam's chest as he lazily brushes his thumb across my nipple. I'm already thumping with arousal, and we've barely recovered from the round we just finished.

"If you keep doing that, I'm never letting you leave," I tell him, rubbing his leg with my foot.

"Fine, I'll stop," he says.

Before I can object, his hand creeps down my belly and between my legs. My head falls back as he thrusts a finger between my legs and I sigh, somehow so satisfied even as his hand renews the yearning for more.

"Should I stop... now?" he asks as his finger circles my clit.

"Nope."

So much steady pleasure, it doesn't seem possible. I can't believe I've missed out on this for so long. I want to stay in bed with him forever, making up for lost time.

As much as I love his touch, I want him inside me. I wish he could live there.

He moves, hovering over me, and I reach down to caress

him. He's hard, and I want him, so I guide him between my legs again. Needing no further instruction, he pushes into me and I feel complete. I spread my knees wider as he moves deeper, closing my eyes and moaning with pleasure.

Slow can be nice, too, apparently. But as we approach the peak of pleasure, our movements are more hurried, harder, faster. I come first, and he follows. He crushes me with his weight again, but I welcome it, wrapping my arms around him.

He's still inside me, my arms still wrapped around him, when I say, "I thought of something you should bring tomorrow night."

"What's that?" he murmurs, eyes still closed.

"Condoms."

He nods, easing out of me and rolls into his side. "I will absolutely get those."

"A big box," I specify.

"The biggest."

I grin, turning and burrowing against him. "It's really cold in here. I need you to stay and keep me warm. So I don't freeze to death. Strictly a matter of life and death."

Liam smirks, and I want to kiss his face again. "I still wish I could and I'm still not going to. You can come up with as many reasons as you want to, the result won't change."

I give him a lazy shrug. "Can't blame a girl for trying."

I wish something would work. Anything. It's scary to think about him leaving again tomorrow, knowing I'll have to go through the same thing. Only tomorrow, I'll know I won't even see him again until after... whatever. And it's undoubtedly dangerous.

"Is Blondie doing whatever it is you're doing, too?"

"Lance? Yeah."

I'm surprised he even answered me. Maybe I can get more information if I come at it the back way. "Are there other people involved, or just you two?"

"More."

"It sounds like a big operation," I guess.

He shrugs. I trace circles on his chest with my finger.

"Why would Raj want me dead?"

Liam sighs heavily. "I don't want to talk about this."

"You're going to kill Pietro, aren't you?"

"Yes."

Finally, something!

"Paul?"

"Oh yes."

I smile, though I'm sure that's probably not the appropriate reaction.

"Others?"

"I've told you enough," he states.

I guess he has, but I ask quietly, "My mom?"

He brushes my hand away and sits up, moving to get out of bed.

I follow, putting a hand in his shoulder. "Okay, I'll stop asking. Stay here and cuddle me."

"I should bring in some more wood," he tells me.

I wrap my arms around his shoulders from behind, and leave a trail of light kisses along his back. "I think there's enough wood."

"In case I'm delayed and you get stuck here for a while, I need to bring in more."

I sit back on my heels. "Is there a good chance that might happen?"

"No, but I want you to be prepared in case."

"So show me where the wood is and I'll bring it in myself if it does," I reason.

Seeming to accept that alternative, he scoots back on the bed. I follow him back in the bed and curl up beside him, pulling the covers over us and basking in his warmth.

"What will you do at the beach house?" I ask him.

"You," he answers, catching my hand and pressing a kiss to my palm.

"Mm, I like the sound of that," I tell him with a grin. "What will I do?"

"Me."

I laugh as he kisses his way up my arm. "I'm serious."

"We'll figure it out once we get settled in. We won't need to work right away. I figure we'll enjoy it for a while, then as long as we both like it, we'll start putting a life together." He stops kissing me, but keeps his hand entwined with mine. "When we leave, we'll be on our own. Just the two of us and whatever we make ourselves."

"Sounds amazing."

"If something changes and you don't like it, don't be afraid to tell me. I'll help you set something up for yourself."

"Trying to get rid of me already?" I tease.

He remains serious. "You've had to depend on others your whole life. You don't anymore. If something changes for you, I don't want you to feel trapped again. I'm not another Paul or Pietro. You're not stuck and you never will be."

Frowning slightly, I say, "I wish you weren't so convinced you're going to scare me off."

"Not convinced. Just making sure you're aware of your options."

"Well, thank you. I think."

He holds me for a while. It's quiet and peaceful. His hand is still in mine, the other lightly moving up and down the area around my shoulder. I want to know what he's thinking, but I doubt he would tell me if I asked.

Turns out, I don't have to.

"Are you close to your brother and sister?"

It's maybe the last question I expected from him.

"Uh... no, not really. I mean, I'm sure they're fine, but obviously I have strained relationships with both of their parents, and that's putting it lightly. We never really got a chance to develop any kind of relationship." I pause a couple seconds. "Do you have siblings?"

"Ryder."

I tilt my head to look up at him, surprised. "Oh, he's your brother?"

He nods, but still looks pensive.

"Are you close to your parents? Do they live around here?"

He shakes his head no.

I'm not sure if it's a sore subject, or he's merely lost in thought. Either way, doesn't seem like I'm going to get much from him.

I hug him extra long before I let him out the door. It's not as hard as it was to let him leave the first time, but it's still hard. It's still scary. I'm still worried about what he's going to be doing and how much danger he'll be putting himself in.

His lips linger on mine for a minute before he pulls away. I want to stall some more, but I understand he stayed as long as he could, and now he has to hustle back.

I don't cry when he leaves this time, but I want to. This cottage is lonely without him, and I can only sweep the dingy floor and wipe down the short, weathered counter so many times. I imagine I'm preparing the house for him to come home to, but knowing this isn't where we'll stay takes away any accomplishment in such busywork.

Daydreams about the future are a little scary, too, but in a good way. What will it be like, just the two of us? No Paul, no Raj, nothing to keep us apart. I've lived with a man before, but I don't know if he's ever lived with someone. There's still so much I don't know about him, so much I want to learn.

I don't want to wait. I don't want there to be a chance for anything else to go wrong.

I call him.

I know it's fruitless, but I also know he's still walking through the woods, so I can.

As soon as he answers, without even a greeting, I ask, "Have you ever lived with a woman before?"

"What?"

"A woman. I mean, that you're in a relationship with."

It sounds like he's pushing through some brush. "Not exactly. Why? You leave the seat up?"

I crack a smile. "No, but I'm really bad at checking mail. Like, really bad. I'll bring it inside, but actually opening it feels like too much work, so I put it somewhere and forget about it. Prepare for some late fees on our bills."

"I don't think it'll be an issue," he says, apparently unconcerned.

"I also keep food, like... days past the expiration date. Two days. Three if I'm living on the edge."

"Oh, well, in that case, never mind."

"I kick in my sleep sometimes."

"Are you trying to talk me *out* of this?" he asks.

I'm quiet for a minute, then I admit, "I'm just kind of afraid you won't like me if I'm around all the time."

Now it's his turn to be quiet. My heart races after the vulnerability I've just exposed. Finally he just says, "Annabelle," in this trailing off, going nowhere kind of way. I don't know exactly what to make of it, but I guess it's supposed to be reassuring.

"We're skipping dating entirely and moving straight to living together. You aren't going to have a chance to see if you even really like me that much," I add, like I can't stop. All of a sudden my insecurities are running out of me like a faucet.

"I do like you," he states. "I wouldn't be doing any of this if I didn't."

"But what if you stop?"

"Then you can kick me in bed and pretend you were sleeping."

I crack a smile. "I'm serious."

"Please stop worrying about this," he says. "We have enough legitimate shit to worry about right now, you worrying that I'm not going to like you enough to live with you doesn't make the cut. I think about you all the time. I want you with me all the time. Now you will be."

That last part is reassuring. He's not the most emotionally open guy in the universe, so I'm pleased to know he *does* like me.

"Oh, good," I say, breathing a little easier. "That makes me happy. I feel the same way."

"Good. We're going to have plenty of time after this is all

over to get to know each other better. If you don't like me, you can always leave. Right now I'm about to get in the car and I don't want you to waste your charge, so I'm gonna go. But I'll be back soon, and then we can talk about this more if you need to."

I smile, further pleased. "Okay, good. Thank you."

He chuckles and ends the call before I can add, "Be safe."

CHAPTER TWENTY THREE
Liam

I've got the truck in my sights. Outside of it, shadowy men keep shifting around. One is puffing on a cigarette and looking around, the other just stands under the streetlight with his arms crossed, posture tense.

I check my phone, but it's quiet.

Something doesn't feel right.

These guys are just hanging around the truck—where's the buyer?

My phone finally buzzes and I read the message on the display.

"Ready?"

I want to abort the mission. Something seems off and this wasn't in my job description anyway. I did this bonus work the first time because seeing how they treated Annabelle pissed me off and I wanted Pietro to pay any and every way he could, but I'm not into it tonight. I don't want to put myself at risk causing more damage, I just want to fulfill my original contract and go back to Annabelle.

That's a foreign thought to pass through my mind, but there it is.

I want to go home. Not to the cabin or my shitty apartment, but to wherever she is.

Annabelle's my home now. I couldn't explain to her how ridiculous her concerns about me not wanting to live with her were, since I don't have any logical explanation to offer, but… somehow it happened.

I can feel myself changing in response to her coming into my life, and I don't know what to do about it. Maybe nothing. Maybe let it happen.

That's pretty scary in and of itself.

Sighing, I shove the phone in my pocket and drop the binoculars in the open window of my car door. They fall on the seat and I creep up toward the hood, waiting on the help that should be coming.

Electricity suddenly fires into my lower back and every tendon in my body strains as my muscles contract painfully. White hot pain disables my body and overtakes my mind. I grunt, toppling to the hood of my car, and while pain still radiates through my body, several sets of hands grab me, holding me down and securing my hands behind my back with a zip tie.

I turn my head to establish who's attacking me and see the smug face of Pietro Basso, which I expected, and the dark, slightly smiling face of Raj Ahuja, which I did not.

Another jolt of electricity shoots into my back and my head swims, my muscles screaming in pain. I try to move, though I'm not sure what I could do at the moment, but I can't anyway. My muscles are useless as I slump helplessly against the hood of my beat-up car.

Threats and curses fly through my head before someone

strikes me in the back of the head, and everything goes black.

I don't know how long I was out, but when my eyes open it's clear I've been stowed somewhere.

I'm confused. I don't know why I'm alive. I'm tied to a chair with my hands not only zip tied, but also secured with rope, and I'm in a windowless, cement-block room. The only light is an exposed bulb over by the door with a pull-string to turn it off and on.

Raj sits in a rusted folding chair by the door. Just the sight of him sets my blood to boiling.

I jerk my hands intuitively, and even though I'm clearly not getting loose, he jumps a little.

Trying to cover it up, he shifts in his seat, scoots around a little. He settles with his hands together, nervously running his thumb across his knuckles.

"Liam," he acknowledges.

"What the *fuck*?" I growl.

He sits forward, his eyes meeting mine across the small room. "I'm sure you have a lot of questions. Forget them. Listen to me, because I'm sure you want to kill me right now. I'm sure you're foaming at the mouth, waiting for your chance to tell Pietro what you know about me. If you do, I'll kill Annabelle."

"Bullshit." If he knew where Annabelle was, and he's working with Pietro for whatever reason, there's no reason I'd be alive.

He's not as good at this as he must think he is, because I see the fear jump in his eyes.

"Everything is still going to go according to plan, just without you. I couldn't trust you. *You* made it impossible to trust you. You lied to my face and you took that goddamn girl—"

"Spare me the monologue," I say with a sneer. "I don't give a fuck."

He sits back, looking a little put out. I imagine him rehearsing the satisfying speech he's going to deliver in front of his mirror, his soft, bare chest all puffed up.

Ha, fuck this guy.

"Was she worth it?" he asks solemnly.

"Really?" I respond, not trying to hide my scorn.

He's going with "was she worth it?" I'm not his estranged husband, for fuck's sake.

Pushing to his feet, obviously annoyed with me, Raj says one last time, "Tell Pietro you were working for me and Annabelle dies. Especially if Pietro kills me before I can do it." Smiling a sick little smile, he adds, "Maybe he'll let her husband have her back for a few days first."

My lips curl up in disgust and I make a show of lurching forward, rattling the chair I'm tied to.

Finally opening the door, Raj flees to tell Pietro I'm awake.

The door rattles before it's jerked open.

Pietro Basso steps through, his smarmy smile and immaculate gray suit out of place in the bleak, dingy room. It's disappointing that these are the circumstances. I thought if I ever saw Pietro Basso in person, it would be to shoot him as he tried to flee his burning house.

Instead, he gets to kill me.

Clasping his hands together theatrically, Pietro says, "At long last, we meet."

I keep my eyes on him, steady, unimpressed, but not angry. He'd love me angry.

"Are you excited?" he continues, still grinning. "I'm excited."

I'm not giving him anything. In fact, I may not utter a single word to him. We'll see how it plays out.

"Man of few words, huh? That's okay. We can get right down to business."

Pietro glances down at the seat, briefly unimpressed with the state of it, but he sits anyway. Slapping his hands on top of his thighs, he tones his grin down to a smile. "So. What've you got for me?"

I don't bother answering, not like he expects me to. Maybe with a fuck you, but not a real answer.

"Let's start with the obvious. Where'd you take Annabelle? Liam, was it?" he asks, glancing back through the door. Raj lingers outside, glancing my way before looking back to Pietro with a nod.

"Liam," Pietro says with a nod-and-smile. "You wouldn't believe how long I've waited to know your name. Silly, isn't it? Anyway. Here you are now, so let's make this as quick and painless as we can, hm?"

I hadn't planned on dying when I took this job, but sitting here looking at this polished sleazebag, I'm still not sorry I did. Annabelle would've wasted away her whole life, trapped under the thumb of this asshole and other assholes like him. Not like I was doing a whole hell of a lot with my life anyway. Still rather live than die, but... I'm glad I saved her, even if this is where it got me.

I sure wish I would've listened to her and stayed home though. Taken off to the beach house with her. Apparently fucking Raj had someone else who could finish the job without me, so he would've even cleaned up my mess.

I'd gotten too comfortable. You do this kind of thing long enough, you take for granted that you've gotten away with it. Seems like you'll always get away with it, even if you know there's a chance you won't.

"No?" Pietro says, like there was any other answer. He doesn't seem concerned though, and as I watch him extract my cell phone from his pocket, I realize why.

Something cold slithers down my throat, sinking down my torso. My face remains stoic, but I know before he says anything that I fucked up.

I didn't erase the number Annabelle called me from earlier.

I want to punch myself in the fucking face. What kind of rookie-ass mistake is it not to clear the call log? Fucking seriously.

My mind races but comes up empty of ideas. I could change the subject, tell him where the stuff Raj had us steal is hidden.

Of course Raj may have moved it, since apparently Raj is on both sides. And obviously he set me up, so he would know there was a chance I'd do that.

I could send him on a wild goose chase. That'd serve Pietro right.

I'm not going to have time to do any of that though, because Pietro is making a call now. I want to stop him, but I'm hoping for a miracle—that she's not by the phone, that she's sleeping the day away like she does sometimes, that she doesn't call back and he'll never know for sure it was her.

But then he grins like a fucking wolf and drawls, "Annabelle. We've missed you."

CHAPTER TWENTY FOUR
Annabelle

The playful smile that popped up when I saw Liam's number has melted away, leaving dull horror in its place. I can't breathe.

I pull back the phone with shaky hands to reread the display.

Liam's number.

Pietro's fucking voice.

They've caught Liam.

Maybe they didn't. Maybe there's another explanation. There *has* to be another explanation.

I swallow hard, putting the phone to my ear. I open my mouth to speak, but nothing comes out. I don't want to speak. I don't want him to hear my voice, even though I know he already did when I answered.

Happy. Excited. Expecting Liam. In the middle of imagining the new life we were about to build together, far away from all this bullshit.

No more beach house.

No more future.

No more Liam.

Tears burn behind my eyes as that dream slips away. I should've known better. Helplessness takes root again, blackening everything it touches inside of me.

I can't do this again.

Pietro's voice through the phone makes my skin crawl. "Annabelle, I'm afraid I've got some bad news."

Oh, God. He's going to tell me Liam's dead.

My legs are sacks of jelly and can't keep me up anymore. I drop hard onto the red plaid couch where I watched Liam's beautiful, strong body hunched to build a fire to keep me warm.

"Your boyfriend tried to steal from me again. I'm afraid it didn't go well for him." There's some static and the line cuts out for a second. "You wanna say hi?"

My heart practically explodes and relief pours through my body. "He's alive?"

"For now," Pietro replies.

"Let me talk to him," I demand.

He puts me on speaker. "Go on, say hi."

Nothing.

I wait. Strain to listen. I want to crawl through the phone, but there's nothing, no sign of Liam.

The silence drags on *forever*.

A little less cheerful, Pietro says, "He's not terribly chatty, is he?"

"Liam?" I question. It's not lost on me that Pietro could be lying. Maybe Liam isn't there—but is it because he didn't actually catch him, just got his phone somehow? Or is Liam dead?

If he's there, he doesn't answer me.

Pietro sighs. A muffled, "Go get Antonio."

I don't know Antonio's purpose but it can't be good, and my stomach is furious at this whole situation. I want to hang up, but I can't until I know if he really has Liam.

I have no idea what to do if he doesn't. Drive myself crazy waiting to see if Liam shows up at this godforsaken cabin? Wait for Pietro's goons to find me? I know they have no way of tracking me from this phone call—that's the whole reason Liam gave it to me, but….

What do I do if Liam's really gone?

And what the hell do I do if he isn't?

"Remember I said we'd do this as painlessly as possible?" Pietro says, but not to me. "Last chance. Talk to Annabelle."

Nothing.

I frown, not knowing what to expect. What to trust. Is Pietro putting on a show for me, or is he actually talking to Liam? If Liam's there, why won't he say so?

Unless he doesn't want me to know.

Of course he doesn't want me to know.

"Liam?" I ask, tentatively. "Please don't try to be a hero right now. I want to know if you're there."

Still nothing.

There's commotion on the other end. Then a noise I can't quite identify, something hitting something, maybe?

Pietro speaks up. "Unfortunately I can't promise your lover's state will be as previously stated for much longer. He doesn't want to talk, so we're giving him a little… incentive."

I think I make out a weak grunt, but with the sound of something striking… something?

My grip tightens on the phone. "Are you *hitting* him?"

"With a pipe," Pietro responds cheerfully.

"Stop! Jesus Christ, stop!" I jump off the couch, full of useless adrenaline. I don't want to cede to any demands when I'm not even sure they have him, but I also don't want them to beat him to death if they do.

"He's not talking yet."

"That's—I don't care. I believe you! Stop hurting him." The striking sound ceases and I can picture Pietro, holding a well-manicured hand up, all smug and fucking disgusting.

"What do you want?" I ask lowly.

"It's not so much what I want as what your mother wants," Pietro replies. "She wants you back home. She wants you at the party with all the relatives who expect to see you there, being the dutiful fucking daughter that you are not. I'm done with these games, Annabelle. I'm done letting you hurt your mother. It's time to come home, it's time to make nice, it's time to put all this bullshit behind you."

Every shred of me rejects what he's saying, but I have to help Liam. I never thought I'd get out—now I have and Pietro is trying to drag me back.

"What do I get out of this deal?" I'm surprised by the evenness, the calm sound of my voice. You'd never know I want to vomit and cry and hit something all at once.

"You won't have to go back to Paul," he states. "He's already moved on. We can begin divorce proceedings as soon as the last of the guests leave and this goddamned party is behind us."

"And Liam?"

"Is dangerous," he states.

He won't let him go. Even if I surrender myself and go back, he's never going to let Liam out alive. He can't. I know that.

I close my eyes, desperately shuffling through my brain for any idea.

"If you let us go, if you let us leave, we'll both disappear and you'll never see us again. We'll never bother you again."

"I'm sure," he says, almost amused.

"I'm serious. Liam was doing this for me. He doesn't give a damn about you. There's no undying vengeance or whatever, he doesn't... it doesn't matter. If you'll just let us be together..."

He pauses. Maybe he's considering it.

Finally, slowly, he says, "All right. *After* the party. You'll show up for your mother, put in one last performance, and afterward I'll let you both go. If I ever see either one of you again, you'll die on sight."

"You won't," I rush out. "You won't. You'll never see us again."

"Good." He doesn't even miss a beat. "Where are you? I'll send a car for you."

I look out the small bedroom window at the trees outside. "Um, I'm not really sure. There's not an address or anything. Hold on, I think... I think there's one of those longitude and latitude readers in here somewhere. If I can find it, would you be able to figure out where I am?"

"Yes," he answers, smoothly.

"Annabelle, don't you fucking dare."

My heart jumps at the sound of Liam's voice. Then sinks, because he really *is* there and I don't know if that's better or worse than the alternative.

"Liam," I cry. "Are you okay? Where are you?"

"He's lying to you, Annabelle. Don't you *dare* tell them where you are."

"Shut him up," Pietro says.

"No! Don't," I object.

"I'm already dead," Liam states. "Don't you dare come back. Get the hell out of here. Do what I told—"

He gets cut off, I hear signs of a scuffle and I feel so.

Fucking. Helpless. "Don't you hurt him!" I scream.

The noise on the other end tapers off as my heart hammers around in my chest.

"I have a stipulation," I add, inspired. "I want him to come to the party with me."

Pietro laughs.

"I'm serious. You can drug him if you have to, those drugs like you gave me. To make him… harmless, but I want him there. It will make more sense when we disappear after anyway. If he's my date. It'll make sense to Mom. What are you going to tell *her* when we disappear?"

He doesn't respond immediately. Maybe he took the bait.

"It'll make sense to everyone. I ran off with Liam. That makes sense, right? I would do that. I *did*."

Because I believe that we'll disappear after the party—he'll kill us. Both of us. I'm more trouble than I'm worth, and Liam's too dangerous. He has no reason to keep either one of us alive.

"I'll play the part. I'll be pleasant at the party. I'll keep Liam under control." I let my voice drop, falter a bit. "Just let Liam be my date, that way… that way we get one last day together." I miss a beat before adding, "Before you let us go, I mean."

He doesn't immediately respond and I'm antsy. Do I add an imploring, "Please?" or is that too much?

Then Pietro says, "All right. On the condition that you convince him to tell me where the stolen shit is, I'll let you do that."

"I will," I promise, not having to feign my eagerness. I could give a fuck less about stolen drugs, but if Liam *does* still have something Pietro wants, and he figures I can get the information for him, that gives me hope he'll actually keep Liam alive.

"I'll need to see Liam," I tell him. "I want to know he's okay before I… turn myself in," I say, for lack of better word.

"You just heard him talking, didn't you?"

"I'll need to know he's *still* okay," I specify. "We'll meet somewhere in the morning."

"That's not what we agreed on."

"If I tell you where I am, you can retrieve me, willing or not. I need to know Liam stays alive. That's the only reason I'm doing this, and if you hurt him, I'll run for the hills."

After a moment, he clips, "Fine. We'll meet at Paul's house. Early. Let's call it 8am."

I don't know how I'm going to get there by 8am. I don't know how I'll get there at all. But he doesn't know where I am, so he doesn't know that.

"Fine."

"And Annabelle? If you try anything stupid, I'll kill another man you love, and this time? Right in front of you."

Rage explodes in my veins until I'm shaking with it. I can't speak. My mind is buzzing with blinding white fury.

I want him to die.

The call ends, but I'm rooted to the spot, overcome with loathing. And terror. Because I don't know what I'm doing, and I could be making the biggest—and last—mistake of my life.

But I have to try to save Liam.

He saved me, and this is where it got him.

Pushing my anger away, I try to clear my head. This isn't the time to be emotional. I need to think.

Going to the closet, I pull out the go-bag Liam showed me when we first got here. I dig through it until I come to the little square of paper with a phone number jotted down.

I swallow, staring at it.

I don't know if this person will be able or willing to help me.

I don't even know if he'll believe me.

But I don't know what else to do.

I wonder what time it is wherever he is as I dial the number, but there's no time to worry about it.

One ring. Two rings. Three rings.

My heart pounds. What if he doesn't answer? Will he call back?

A fourth ring and my anxiety intensifies.

Then a husky male voice utters, "Hello?"

I'm partially relieved, but mostly nervous. "Hi. Is this Ryder?"

I don't even know if that's okay to ask. Should I use his name? Should I be more discreet? Is there some kind of code or etiquette I'm unaware of?

"Who wants to know?"

I take that as a yes. "My name's Annabelle. I was… um, I was kind of given your number by Liam. Liam Hunt," I add, more excited than I should be that I know his last name.

"Look, I don't care how blonde or buxom you are, it's 2 o'clock in the goddamn morning and I was asleep."

"I'm neither of those things. Liam's in trouble."

That seems to get his attention. "What?"

"I'm his… girlfriend?" I say, for lack of better word.

"What?" he says again.

"He told me you wouldn't believe me. He told me to ask you how the ladies like the scar he gave you?"

I can hear my own heart beating as I wait for him to say something. I need help and I don't know what I'll do if he doesn't believe me. Or if he does, but there's just nothing he can do.

I *need* to get to that party with Liam by my side. I don't know how, but I'm confident we have a far better shot of getting out alive if we're together.

    Finally breaking the taut silence, Ryder demands, "What happened to Liam?"

CHAPTER TWENTY FIVE
Annabelle

I haven't slept.

Ryder told me to, but I couldn't.

I'd gotten a few hours before Pietro called, and though they burn, my eyes are just going to have to push through this morning, then whatever comes after it.

The sound of a fist pounding against the door startles the hell out of me. It's still dark outside and even though I know it must be Ryder, I can't shake the paranoia that it could be Pietro.

"You awake?"

I'm relieved to hear what must be the voice of the man from the phone.

I open it, a little at first, then enough for him to come inside. The fire died and it's bitterly cold outside. A gust of wind follows him in and chills spring up all over me. I cross my arms over my chest, rubbing my arms, trying to keep warm.

Ryder is tall. That's the first thing I make note of. He's handsome. Smaller than Liam. Tall and lean with brown eyes and a clean-shaven jawline.

He casts a sweeping gaze around the cabin as he comes inside. Don't know what he expected to find, but then his gaze makes it to me. He makes no attempt to disguise his brief perusal, apparently appraising the woman Liam decided was worth risking his life for.

I can't tell if he's impressed or not. These guys don't give much away when it comes to what they're thinking.

"Ready to go?" he asks.

I nod, glancing around the room uncertainly. I have Liam's go-bag and some granola bars I tossed inside, but I don't know if we'll ever be back here. I don't know if there's anything I should take.

"Were you able to get that guy?"

He said he might be able to call on someone local for help.

Ryder nods. "He's meeting us with a car." Then, taking a moment to actually check on me, he asks, "Are you ready to do this?"

"I have no idea," I tell him, shaking my head.

"You were raised around mobsters, weren't you?"

"Adjacent to them. I was never involved. I was certainly never raised to participate in shit like this myself."

He cracks a smile and heads back out the door. "You'll be okay."

I don't know how these magicians navigate the woods here, but I'm more than a little winded trying to keep up.

After I explained the situation to Ryder on the phone, he sort of took over the planning. He said he'd try to contact a guy who might be able to get here fast, and he'd bring a car for me since I obviously couldn't be dropped off.

So many conflicting emotions war within me as we trek through these woods. It's early so I'm freezing my ass off while Ryder hikes like a mountain man. I manage not to fall and we make it to the car much more quickly than when Liam brought me out here.

It's not blustery once I get into the white car I assume is his. The car is quiet as he backs out onto the road and I stare out the window, thinking of what's ahead of us.

Glancing at him uncertainly, I ask, "So, what's the plan?"

"Ideally I'm hoping we all make it out alive," he says, brightly, maybe a little sarcastically.

I'm sure he blames me for Liam's predicament, so I just watch out the windshield for a few miles.

When he still doesn't fill me in, I sigh. "Look, whether you like me or not, I need to know what the plan is so I can help."

"Seems like you've helped plenty," he says with a deceptively light and playful wink.

That kind of pisses me off. "I *begged* him not to go back there. I'm not to blame here, and I'm going to do whatever has to be done to save him. I didn't have to call you. If I didn't care about Liam, I would've taken the money he left me and disappeared, wouldn't I?"

"I doubt you know how to," he muttered, but without much spunk.

A couple of silent minutes later, Ryder says, "Tell me about this house we're meeting him at."

I'm not sure exactly what he wants to know, so I tell him everything I can think of. The layout, how close the neighbors are, the thicket of trees behind it. I tell him how many windows I can recall, which one Liam came in through.

The problem is there are so many things we *don't* know, which makes it difficult to form a solid plan. I don't know how many men Pietro will have when we get there. I don't know what kind of reception I'll get once I'm in their grasp. I should've probably made him agree to meet me somewhere public, like the deli, instead of at Paul's house. There's not much in the way of protection if Pietro decides the missing drugs aren't worth the risk and he just has me killed right away.

There are *so many* unknowns.

Will he even have Liam? Once I'm there, there's nothing I can do if they don't. As soon as he can see me, he can send men to grab me.

We're working on the honor system here, and Pietro has no honor.

Ryder's voice pulls me out of my depressing thoughts.

"We want to grab him today. There's no guarantee your stepfather keeps his word. Liam may not even make it to the party, and he sure as hell isn't going to let you bring him with you. Once you're inside I'm not going to be able to communicate with you, so I won't be able to let you in on whatever plan I manage to come up with. Nothing about this is going to be easy."

I nod my understanding. I'm dreading this so much and so nervous about it all that I feel physically ill. If we had time, I'd ask Ryder to stop at a gas station so I could throw up.

We're halfway there when my cell phone rings.

My gaze jerks to Ryder and he nods silently.

Heart in my throat, I answer, "Hello?"

"Change of plans."

It's not Pietro. It's Paul.

Resentment pours out of me as I snap, "Why?"

"Because I fucking said so, that's why."

"Because Pietro said so, you mean," I correct him.

I hope he feels like the little fucking lapdog he is.

"You really wanna be a bitch to me when I have your *hero*'s life in my hands?"

I want to punch him in the face while hurting the hell out of his ego, but I guess this isn't the time.

"What's the change?" I ask.

"We're meeting in Paterson. Red brick warehouse, has a big, old banner hanging across the front that says 'now hiring'. You'll pull in the driveway on the left and come through the open door."

"Wait, Paterson?" I question, looking to Ryder. "What warehouse? I don't know how to get there."

Ryder is scowling.

"I'll text you the address, just put it in the GPS on your phone and—"

"I don't *have* GPS on this phone."

"Jesus Christ, Annabelle. Google it then! It's not that hard."

"I don't like this. Is Liam there?"

"Yes," he snaps. "And if you really want to see him, you'll fucking get here."

"Why can't we just meet at the house like we planned?"

He doesn't answer, and it takes me a minute to pull back the phone and see the call has ended. Bastard hung up on me.

"What's going on?" Ryder asks.

With a sinking stomach, I tell him, "They've changed the location to a warehouse in Jersey. I don't know why."

"To show they're in control, probably." He says it casually, but that makes me uneasy. Pietro isn't an insecure guy and he's obviously in control—why would he feel the need to prove that?

"He said... he said if I try anything stupid, he'll kill Liam," I tell him, knowing that calling him for help is exactly the kind of stupid thing he was referring to.

He's matter-of-fact. "Of course he will. If we don't get him out of there, they *will* kill him. They didn't kidnap him so they'd have an extra dinner guest."

It doesn't seem to bother him, but it bothers me. What if

they figure out he's there? I didn't know where he was going to hide before, and that was when I knew the layout. I've never been to this warehouse. I have no clue what's around it or how Ryder will be able to keep an eye on anything.

I'm starting to realize this is hopeless.

"What if we can't save him?" I hate to voice it, but we're also running out of time. "What if I'm turning myself over to these monsters for nothing?"

He looks over at me but doesn't respond. His gaze returns to the road, and after a few seconds he says, "I'm going to do my best not to let that happen. Whether Liam makes it or not, I won't abandon you in there. It's not what Liam would've wanted."

The way he says it, like Liam's already gone, sends chills down my spine.

CHAPTER TWENTY SIX
Annabelle

The sky is gray and devoid of light. Dark clouds have gathered. The wind whips violently as I pull into the driveway to the left of the abandoned warehouse in Paterson.

I'm terrified this is the last thing I'll ever see. I grip the steering wheel, looking up at all three levels. I don't see any of Pietro's men yet. There's a red door on each level, and the one on the bottom floor is hanging open.

Placing a hand to my stomach, willing it to calm down, I search for placidity. I've done this before. I've done this so many times. I can find it in me to fake my way through one more bout with these assholes.

My stomach just doesn't agree.

My nerves feel all fluttery but I'm not going to get anywhere sitting in my car. I have to get out eventually. If I don't, they'll just come get me.

I'm here now.

There's no going back from here.

I have to hope something good comes out of this, because whatever waits for me on the other side of that red door, I'm going to have to face it alone.

Pushing the car door open, I climb out on shaky legs. Flashes of my life come back to me, flashes of Paul, of curling up in a dark room under blankets, crying by myself. As much as I want to save Liam, I can't shake the feeling that I'm crazy for being here.

I pad up the stretch of concrete, searching for movement. Nothing.

I really, really don't want to, but I push the red door the rest of the way open. It creaks and I grimace, my eyes darting around as if the sound may have summoned someone.

The lights aren't on inside and the vast, shadowy space does nothing to ease my jittery nerves.

I don't know where to go. My steps slow and I look around for direction.

There's still no one so I keep walking toward the back, toward more doors.

Nervous butterflies ravage my insides, worse with each step I take. The urge to turn around and run is so strong, I almost do it.

I don't know which door to choose once I reach them. I'm torn between not wanting to announce my presence, and wanting to call out and get it over with.

I pick a door at random—the third—and push it open. It opens into another dark, narrower space. It's chilly inside, obviously no heat, and I want to leave. So badly.

I follow the hall around a corner and it's narrower again, this time with doors all down the corridor on the left and right.

"You've gotta be kidding me," I whisper to myself.

I decide to turn back.

Before I make it back around the corner, however, I hear a door open and close behind me.

Spinning around, I move my back closer to the wall.

It's Paul.

Fucking Paul.

He smiles when he sees me, and proceeds to meander after me like he doesn't have a problem in the world. I guess, with me gone, maybe he doesn't.

"There's my stunning wife," he mocks.

I remember Pietro promising I won't have to go back with Paul. His word may be flimsy at best, but it's all I've got.

"Where is he?" I call to him, uncomfortable that he's coming closer.

"Pietro?"

"Liam."

Some of the smugness on his face falls, bitter resentment slipping into its place. "Thor's been grounded."

I resist the urge to taunt him. "I want to see him. That was the deal."

"Oh, you'll see him," he assures me, giving me the creeps.

He's right in front of me now, and even though I refuse to be afraid of him, my stomach somersaults.

I don't want his hands on me, but he reaches out to grab me by the arm. I resist, out of habit, gritting my teeth and glaring at him.

Paul smiles.

Not releasing my arm, he tugs me along. I follow because I want to see Liam, but I jerk my arm free as soon as his grip eases up.

Warily eyeing the door, I make note of all the locks. Most of the doors I've seen before this one don't have locks at all, or if they do, just a simple twist lock on the knob. This one has 4 additional locks installed. Not for keeping someone out, I suspect, but for keeping someone in.

My heart kicks up several speeds as he shoves the door open.

It's a dark, rectangular room with cinderblock walls. There's a generic exposed light bulb just inside the room, and in the small space to the left I see Greg, Pietro, and Antonio.

I look to the right and see my Liam, bruised, dirty, with cuts on his face and a swollen lip, but all in one piece. He looks terrible and wonderful and he's tied to a chair.

I don't think, I just run to him, kneeling on the cold cement floor before him as tears spring to my eyes.

He's hurt, but he's alive.

He looks both furious and happy to see me.

"Liam," I whisper, my hands thoughtlessly kneading his thighs. He flinches just slightly and I frown, confused.

Then I remember about the pipe. The beating. I don't know where, I couldn't see.

My hands lighten on the tops of his thighs. I was so afraid for him, I can't stand not touching him, but I'm almost afraid to. I don't want to hurt him, but I also want to throw myself into his arms and feel safe.

But I won't be.

Liam can't keep me safe right now. It's all on me.

"I wish you wouldn't have come," he says, miserably.

"I had to," I tell him. "I wasn't going to leave you."

"Touching," Paul says from behind me.

He's close, so I tense.

When he fists a hand in my hair and practically rips it out of my scalp, I'm not even surprised.

Thankfully, *finally*, I feel the reluctant gate in my mind slide back into place, making me a fortress again, out of Paul's reach.

When I rise up off the floor and he jerks me around to meet

his gaze, I'm smiling.

He fists his hand tighter so it hurts more and my smile widens. "You must've missed me, huh? Is Marlene boring? She always struck me as boring. I bet she never gives you an excuse to manhandle her, huh?"

The familiar fury dances in the depths of his muddy brown eyes, but here, now, he isn't impotent with it anymore.

He slams me against the brick wall, hurting my left shoulder with the impact, but I don't lose my smile.

But then *he* smiles. Glances back at Liam, his features and muscles tense with anger.

Then Paul swoops in. I rear back but my back connects with cold, hard wall and there's nowhere to go. His face moves closer and I'm horrified, my gaze jerking to Liam. I don't know why I did that. Realizing Liam is watching makes it *so much worse* as Paul grabs me and smashes his mouth against mine.

As he rips open Liam's old jacket, tears the neck of my sweater, and puts his hands on my breasts.

I try to bring my knee up to smash him between the legs, but I've done that before so he anticipates it and blocks me.

I hear Liam's chair rattling behind Paul. My heart pounds and I turn my face left and right, trying to get his disgusting, wormy little lips off me.

Paul's laughing as he pulls back, and I'm so fucking angry, I shove him hard in the shoulder. I can't look at Liam. I want to. I want to rip off his restraints and watch him tear Paul apart.

"All right," Pietro calls, finally stepping forward and moving closer to us. He acts calm, but I watch him quickly double check Liam's restraints.

From a distance, of course.

Liam seethes wordlessly in his chair. I wonder why he isn't

threatening them.

Then again, Liam doesn't make threats. He delivers on them.

Flicking a glance at my exposed bra, Pietro meets my gaze and smiles.

I feel dirty, so I pull the jacket around me and cross my arms.

"I don't suppose either of you are ready to tell me where my supply is yet?" he inquires, glancing back at Liam.

Liam skewers him with a glance.

Pietro nods. "I figured. That's okay." Then he turns, nodding to Greg. Greg disappears through the door and I frown, wondering where he's going. Dreading where he's going.

"You two get to have a little sleepover. My treat," Pietro states, mockingly generous.

Greg wheels in a cot—a hard metal frame on wheels with a thin, white mattress on top.

Pietro's vacant gaze meets mine. "Strip down or Paul will help you."

"What?" I ask, hoping I somehow misunderstood him.

Behind Greg, Antonio approaches with ropes in his hands.

"We'll have to restrain you as well, obviously," Pietro explains. "Can't have you trying to loose Liam. I'm not sure if you realize, but we've *really* pissed him off," he says, offering a hollow grimace. "You'll spend the night, and when we come back, Liam here will tell me where he put the shit he stole from me."

Paul comes forward, grabbing my jacket. I resist, but then I don't want him to rip it.

"Why do I have to strip down?" I ask. "You're not capable of restraining me with my clothes on?"

"Paul's going to keep guard," Pietro explains, barely able to hold back a smirk. "Keep you company."

I want to be wrong, but I know what he's threatening.

I know what Paul will do.

In front of Liam.

Bile actually rises up my throat. I take a breath, willing the impulse away, but I'm really afraid I'm going to vomit.

I swallow convulsively and only seem to further trigger my gag reflex. I stifle the retching my body so desperately wants to do, but I can still feel it in my throat.

"This wasn't our deal," I tell him, like that means something.

"Yeah. But I make the rules, sweetheart. Not you."

"Please don't do this," I say, pride be damned. I've survived plenty of abuse from Paul, but the thought of his hands on me, his mouth on me... worse things I can't even stand to think about, especially knowing Liam will be tied to a chair, helpless to stop Paul from hurting me.

Forced to watch. To listen.

"You could just tell me now," Pietro suggested, glancing to Liam. "Save Annabelle some... pain and suffering?"

Liam meets my gaze, features steady, but eyes pleading. I'm sure he wants me to understand why he won't fold and save me. He doesn't need to show his hand even that much though; I trust him completely. I know he will do what's best.

I know once Pietro has the information he wants, we're both as good as dead.

Maybe he would keep us alive until he could verify, but once he did....

My stomach roils in protest but my brain understands. I raise my head high, push away the moment of pleading. Whatever they dole out, I can take.

Pietro's dramatic pause ends. "No? All right, then."

"Wait," I say, glancing at the bed. Before they can tie me up, before I'll be as helpless as he is, I hurry over to Liam. It's not the easiest position to work with, but I brace myself on the arms of the chair and lean in, brushing my soft lips across his swollen ones. I want him so badly, so deeply, in every way, and I need this to get through the next day.

Liam does, too. His kiss, even without hands, is passionate, desperate, mind-numbing. His tongue sweeps into my mouth, running along the inside of my lower lip. I savor the taste of him, the feel of him. This is what our days should be filled with. This is how every one of our nights should end. No fear, not being bullied, trussed up and controlled by evil bastards. This.

It feels like a last kiss should.

Paul drags me away, breaking the kiss. I don't fight him. I climb onto the cot, chilled to the bone, but I don't complain.

Paul uses the rope to tie me to the bed and smirks like he's accomplished something.

I'm naked and afraid. The dank, empty warehouse does nothing to warm me as I lie there in a bra and panties, shivering.

I'm finally with Liam, but in these circumstances, I'd almost prefer to be alone.

I want a blanket more than I ever have in my life. It seems excessively cruel that they haven't given me one, and I decide it's probably Paul's doing. He knows my blanket cocoons are my safe place. He wouldn't want me to have that here.

I think of Ryder and that other guy—Al, I think. I don't know where they are or if they were able to find a place close enough. Who knows if they even know where I'm at, and if they do, will they put their own necks on the line to help? And if so, when?

My future is lost in an ocean of uncertainty.

There's nothing and no one I can depend on—this time, not even myself.

CHAPTER TWENTY SEVEN
Annabelle

"This is so romantic, isn't it?" Paul asks, trailing the back of his index finger across my collar bone.

"Fuck off and die," I reply blandly, the embodiment of boredom.

"I mean, we never tried exhibitionism before," he says, like I haven't spoken. His hand moves down my chest, skirting dangerously close to the cup of my bra.

Liam's voice jolts me out of the absent state I'm trying to head into.

"I'm gonna stop you right there, Paul. Turn around. Look at me."

Paul doesn't lose his cocky little fucking smile, but it weakens and he does glance back at Liam. "You want some popcorn?"

Liam is doing his scary stoic thing, and he meets Paul's gaze with detached calm. "Do you recall that night I had your throat beneath my boot and I warned you that if you ever put another unwanted hand on Annabelle again, I'd kill you dead?" He lifts his eyebrows, ever so slightly. "I'm going to warn you right now—and please, *please* don't think I'm exaggerating or being in any way facetious, because I mean this very literally. If you put your puny dick anywhere *near* Annabelle, when I get out of this chair I am going to rip it off and feed it to you." He remains calm, but reiterates, "I will *literally* grab your dick, rip it off your body, put the flaccid, bloody remains in your mouth, and make you chew it." As if to illustrate his point, he gnashes his teeth.

I don't think I've ever appreciated my big, beautiful sociopath more.

Paul chuckles, but I know him well enough to know it's a nervous one. Glancing back at me, he says, "Man, this guy's got no chill, does he?"

"None," I verify.

"Look, man. I don't even *want* Annabelle anymore," Paul informs Liam. "I'm the one who left her. I... I'm in a committed relationship."

"Good," Liam says evenly.

Neither of us bothers to ask how the person he's so committed to would appreciate him feeling me up or forcing a kiss on me a few minutes ago, but I'm content to let that one go.

I don't want to see Paul's dick ever again, bloody or otherwise.

His fun spoiled, it doesn't take long for Paul to grow bored of guarding us. When he opens the door to step outside, I hear feet shuffling and a voice. Antonio is outside the door. They must've put an extra guard on us, in case Paul wasn't sufficient.

Good thinking.

Paul is a lot of things, but rarely sufficient.

"Why'd you come back?" Liam asks me, now that we're alone.

I want to tell him I didn't come alone, but I don't know if

they can hear us outside the door. I don't know if there are cameras somewhere and I just don't see them. I'm not willing to take that chance.

"They would've killed you," I state.

"They'll still kill me," he points out. "Now they'll kill you, too."

"Maybe."

"The drugs won't keep us alive forever. I may've been able to cow *Paul*," he says, so dismissively I have to smile, "but that's not going to work on Pietro. He's empty inside. He'll hurt you to make me talk, and as soon as I do, we're both dead."

"I know that," I mutter, glancing down at the door.

"So *why*?"

I want to tell him so badly. I want Ryder to be the answer to our prayer, but I don't even know if he is. I don't even know if any of this will work. I could've very well walked into a situation I won't walk out of, and Liam's right—Pietro will inflict horrors on me in an attempt to get the information he wants, and once he realizes nothing will work, he'll call it a loss and we'll both die.

It was quite a gamble, I realize.

But it's done now.

"If you're going to die, at least you won't be alone." Then, pulse quickening, I look back at him and add, "The least I could do was make sure someone you *trust* was with you."

His brows furrow together, then realization dawns on his face. His gaze sharpens, questioning.

I nod as much as I'm able, just a tiny motion, because I'm paranoid. It doesn't seem like the kind of place you could put cameras, but they *did* bug my house.

Liam's whole demeanor changes. He eases back as much as he can—poor guy, he's gotta be so uncomfortable tied up like that—and takes a slow perusal of the room. His eyes move to the high ceilings, the windowless walls, the door with all the extra locks.

Not an ideal spot to break into, I imagine.

And that's if Ryder even knows which building we're in. I sure didn't see him anywhere.

The door opens and Paul slinks back in. I listen as he closes the door and notice they don't lock all the locks when he's inside with us.

Maybe we want him to be inside.

"Do you have a blanket?" I ask, my voice small and delicate, the way Paul thinks he likes. (Really, he likes when I piss him off. But he thinks he likes me delicate.)

Paul snorts, pulling up a folding chair on the other side of the room and planting his ass in it. He pulls his phone out and starts playing around on it.

I sigh, injecting as much despondency as I can into it.

"Shoulda made a better fucking choice," Paul mutters, not looking away from his phone. "You were at home in our bed, you wouldn't be wanting for a fucking blanket, now would you?"

"No," I murmur. "I suppose I wouldn't."

He nods, satisfied. "Thor wasn't such a good fucking pick, now was he?"

I won't fess up to that, not because Liam's here and he may not understand I'm playing Paul, but because that would be too much and I don't want to make Paul suspicious.

Instead I go quiet. Blow out some breaths and shudder from the cold.

It takes somewhere around ten minutes before, muttering a string of foul curses, Paul gets out of his chair and yanks his coat off.

His coat smells like him, but I don't make a face as he drapes it over my body to keep me warm.

I offer a tiny, reluctant smile. "Thank you."

He mutters and walks back over to his chair, but I'm satisfied.

If I need Paul to help keep me alive, I'm pretty sure I can call on the little weasel.

Liam may have thought he was going to kill me, but you don't save a woman from her abusive husband if you're going to let her die anyway.

And you don't give her blankets when she's cold.

It's a long night. What's worse, there's no light or dark, so no real sense of time in here. I don't even know if it's just been a night. The only way we can determine it must be morning is Paul leaving and the changing of the guard outside the door. I don't know who it is, only that it isn't Antonio.

Liam and I chat, but only monotonous stuff, none of the questions we both want answers to.

All we can do is wait, and we don't even know for what.

More time passes.

The door eventually eases open and a stocky guy with a big nose lumbers in with a bottle of water. He regards Liam but doesn't approach him. Instead, he comes over to me and unscrews the lid.

"Drink," he says, tipping the bottle up to my lips.

Relief fills me and I greedily gulp down as much water as I can. It occurs to me that I should make sure I don't drink more than half so Liam isn't shortchanged.

Once he pulls the water away, he glances back at Liam again. "Wanna tell us where the shit is stashed?"

Liam doesn't even glance at the guy.

Big Nose nods his head and moves the water bottle over me, dumping the other half all over my body. I cry out as the icy cold water hits my freezing cold skin and that successfully gets Liam's attention. He still doesn't speak, but cold fury takes up residence in the depths of his beautiful brown eyes.

Smirking, Big Nose tells me, "Stay warm, *Principessa*."

Paul took his jacket when he left so I don't even have that for cover. Cold rivulets of water drip down my side, soaking the mattress beneath me. Violent trembling wracks my body and my stupid teeth chatter no matter how hard I try to control it.

Several seconds pass before Liam asks, "How tight are your ropes?"

My wrists were already irritated from all the rubbing, and to be honest, I hadn't even tried to get out of them. "Tight," I tell him.

"Did you bring your car keys in?"

I turn my head and look down at the pile of discarded clothes. "Yeah. Don't know if they grabbed them, but if not they should be down there."

The chair moves with his efforts and I can only imagine the shape he must be in under that rope.

"Please don't hurt yourself," I said.

His deep, gravelly voice is taut with aggravation. "I'm fucking sick of this."

So am I, but we need to be in the best shape we can when Ryder saves us. *If* Ryder saves us.

He *has* to. All my hopes are pinned on this stranger.

"When's the last time they gave you any water?" I ask, but he doesn't answer. "Don't waste your energy."

"You're freezing."

"I'm fine," I assure him, making a more focused effort not to tremble. It doesn't work, but hey, I tried.

I understand, though. The helplessness bugs me, too—our absolute dependence on someone *hopefully* saving us—it has to be even harder for him.

"When's the last time you depended on someone?" I ask.

I glance at him, unsure how he'll receive such an out-of-the-blue question. Especially one so potentially vulnerable.

A moment passes before he answers. "I can't remember."

My eyebrows rise and I send him a searching frown. "What do you mean?" I ask.

His head shakes slightly but he seems pensive, maybe sifting through memories, maybe just unwilling to share. I wish I could tell. Maybe it doesn't matter, because Ryder won't come and Pietro will kill both of us before it all ends, and we'll both die with no one ever knowing either of our stories—and no one who really cares to, anyway.

Back at the cabin I probably wouldn't have pushed, but here, now, it doesn't make sense to hold back.

"You might as well tell me," I say lightly, despite our situation. "I promise I'll still find you mysterious for however long we get to live."

Ignoring my morbid, possibly true, joke, he says, "I'm not trying to be mysterious, I just... I really can't remember. I must've been a kid," he says, like it's a guess. "I don't know. I always remember knowing I couldn't depend on people. I tried to, I guess, but it always turned out to be a stupid-ass idea and eventually I stopped. I guess I gave people chances to prove me wrong after that, openings, but... it never happened. So I don't really know how you classify that."

I ponder his response for a moment, some of it feeling familiar. I had left openings for my mother, even after my sham wedding, for her to get back in if she tried. But she never tried. At least, not in a way that would've worked. If she had admitted wrongdoing and apologized, maybe then I would've been more receptive, but she skipped those crucial steps.

"I take it you didn't have great parents," I say.

"Didn't really have any. I had a mother for a minute, but she wasn't ready for a kid and dumped me off with her father and step-mom. I pretty much took care of myself and just slept there. I used to steal her cigarettes and trade them to these little assholes at school for their lunch or money — whatever they had that I wanted."

That hurts my heart a little, but I don't show any response since I don't want him mistaking it for pity. "How old were you?"

"Nine, ten, eleven. In sixth grade they got divorced. She moved away. He moved us into this little apartment above a repair shop. I started working down there under the table and learning the way of things. It got easier then. I didn't like stealing so I liked having my own money."

"Did you live with him until you graduated?"

"Nah. He met some other woman and moved in with her. I stayed in the apartment above the shop and worked there until I was old enough to enlist."

I sort of smile. "I knew you were a service guy."

"Once upon a time," he verifies. "Anyway, then I was an adult, so..."

"So you never really had anyone."

"Not really."

"What about relationships? Any serious ones?"

"I don't really have the lifestyle for it," he says, which doesn't surprise me. I *am* surprised, a moment later, when he says, "Eh, that's an excuse. I wasn't so married to the lifestyle I couldn't have changed it, I just... I don't know. It isn't easy to get close to people."

Tenderness surges until I feel like I'm drowning in it. I try to keep a lid on it, but God, I just want to hug him.

"You feel close to me?" I ask, ignoring the scary rush of adrenaline I feel just asking, opening myself up that way.

"You have to ask that?"

"I feel close to you," I reply. "But it's still nice to hear."

He looks a little surly, but it amuses me. "Yes, I feel close to you," he mutters.

I wish we weren't maybe-dying, because I really want to get close enough to tease him. I don't want to right now, not when he's just opened up, but God, I need more time with him. We haven't had enough. Not nearly enough.

"I'm scared," I finally tell him.

"I know," he says, softly. A few seconds pass, then he asks, "Do you think you would've liked me if we would've met under different circumstances? Same people, just... better situation."

I want to immediately say yes, but I think it over for a second first. There are certainly things about him I wouldn't have been psyched about—the whole family legacy thing had put me off violent men, so if I didn't actively need one to save me, it probably would have held less appeal.

But he isn't like them. I know logically he would probably do the same bad things if he had to, because above all, Liam is a man who does what needs to be done... but he has heart, a code, a kind of integrity they all lack. He isn't just blowing through life—

and other people's lives—inflicting pain and suffering because he can. They're so cowardly compared to him. It feels like an insult to even compare them in my mind.

"Yes," I finally say. "If I could've somehow still seen behind your shields, I'm sure I would've."

"I probably wouldn't have let you," he says lightly.

"I would have made you," I inform him, playfully haughty.

"Oh, yeah, you're so forceful." He rolls his eyes.

"Hey, I'm totally scary and intimidating."

"I know you can't tell, but I'm shaking over here."

The exchange has taken my mind off things, but now it wanders to bedroom activities, curiosity about things we didn't have a chance to try. I wonder if he'd like me taking charge.

I wonder if Ryder will come through so I get the chance to find out.

Then I frown, realizing the story he told me about his family didn't include a brother. Had he just left it out in case people were listening? I want to ask, but for the same reason, I don't.

CHAPTER TWENTY EIGHT
Annabelle

I manage to fall asleep despite the unrelenting shaking of my chilled body, so when the ramming sound jerks me awake, I'm initially a little pissed.

Then it hits me—the understanding that something is on the other side, trying to get in. Blood rages through my veins. I inhale sharply, torn between fear and excitement.

It has to be Ryder. Right? The bad guys have keys.

I turn my head toward Liam to see if he's awake, if he somehow knows more than I do. His body is rigid, his eyes alert and trained on the door.

"What's going on?" I whisper.

He doesn't answer. I don't know if he was asleep or awake, but fear cloaks me like a blanket as one certainty settles in: one way or another, things are about to change.

Before we have too long to ponder the kerfuffle outside, the door splinters and bursts open. I strain to look, craning my neck, and my heart explodes, relief and happiness pouring through me.

"Oh my God, he did it," I murmur.

Ryder steps through with his darker skinned companion

right behind him. Ryder is smug, but Ali grins when he sees Liam tied to the chair.

"Oh man." Ali reaches into his pocket, I assume to draw out a knife to cut the ropes, but instead he produces a cell phone and snaps a picture.

"You dick," Liam says, but without censure.

"We're the dicks?" Ryder asks, a dark brow rising. "Here you are trying to die without so much as a goodbye and *we're* the dicks?"

As Ryder approaches Liam and begins cutting him loose, Ali comes over to me, his eyes wandering over my bare body. Without looking at my face, he turns and looks around, spotting the pile of clothes on the ground and picking them up.

He drops them on top of my body, then seems to realize I can't get dressed. Finally, he does extract a pocket knife and a moment later I can move. I expect relief, but my muscles are so sore from being held in the same position, all I can do is stretch, trying and failing to find comfort.

"You didn't bring aspirin, did you?" I mutter, extending my arm up over my head and bending it down toward the middle of my back.

"She's cute," Ryder says, instead of answering me.

"That's a no?" I ask Ali.

"I'm sure we've got some in the carriage," he mocks, lightly.

"If not, we'll send a footman," Ryder adds, winking at me.

"A simple no was a lot to ask for, I realize."

Liam is smirking as his friends pick on me, but all that's forgotten a moment later when Liam, no longer restrained, approaches me. I'm still on the cot, but sitting up. I've managed to pull on my pants, but my upper body is still clad only in a bra. His eyes rake over me possessively, like he's torn between taking inventory and deciding which part of me he's going to devour first.

Eyes still on my body, Liam asks, "What day is it?"

"Saturday," Ryder supplies.

Aggravation flickers in the depths of those beautiful brown eyes. "What time?"

Checking the watch on his left wrist, Ryder replies, "Almost 7:30."

"Shit," Liam mutters, finally meeting my eyes. "Get dressed. We have to go."

I nod, opening the bottom of my shirt and slipping it over my head. As I pull it down past my face, I ask, "Where do we go now?"

I expect him to say another hideaway, the cabin in the woods, maybe the airport. Now that we're free and Liam's friends are here, the dream of going away to the sunset house is no longer lost. We can have a future now. Both of us. Together.

What I do not expect, despite everything that's happened so far, is for him to say, "Pietro's."

My spirits drop. I stare at him as my jaw falls open, and his seems to lock up defensively.

He turns away to brief the guys, and I'm still fucking floored.

Finally I find my voice. "You can't be serious."

He doesn't defend himself, merely looks at me and says, "We've gotta move."

"We need to *leave*. We need to get the hell out of here."

Ryder and Ali exchange glances, but Liam's orders obviously trump mine and they walk out the door first.

Liam pushes me ahead of him and I walk out, but I can't *believe* he would even think of going back. Not after all this. Not after we could've both died because he didn't let it go the first time.

"Liam, why would we go there?" I ask quietly, since I figure maybe he's just being a stupid idiot guy in front of his friends. Guys are supposed to be prone to that, right? I hadn't experienced it firsthand since high school (since Paul's *always* an idiot, friends or no) but I was sure that was a thing. Liam being a man with a lot of pride, I figure it's possible.

"The party starts in a half hour."

Of course I knew that when Ryder said what day and time it was, but I don't know why we care.

Fear wraps itself around my stomach and I grab Liam's wrist to get his attention. It works. Those brown eyes burn a hole right through me, delivering passionate declarations without a single syllable falling from his lips.

"This is our chance to run," I implore, quietly. "To start a life together, away from all this."

I want this to work—to remind him how close we came to losing everything, to want me more than he wants... whatever the hell it is he wants.

But I don't expect it to. I expect him to retreat, to pull away from me. I'm relieved when he doesn't. Instead, he leaves my hands wrapped around his wrist and he stops in the middle of the hallway to look me in the eye.

"I have to finish this, Annabelle. I *want* to finish this."

"More than you want to be safe and happy with me?" I ask.

Regret surfaces then and he captures my hand, extracting his wrist from my hold. My stomach bottoms out, expecting him to pull away *now*, but instead he brings my hands to his lips and leaves a gentle kiss there.

"There's nothing I want more than to erase all of the bad

shit that's ever been done to you. I don't have the power to do that... but I *do* have the power to erase the people who did it."

Every hair on my body prickles, goose bumps rising up all over. A desire so deep I'm not even sure I can call it that suddenly blankets me and I'm nearly overwhelmed by the tenderness.

This man, this wonderful, ruthless, mystery of a man... he loves me.

You don't risk your life to slay dragons for a woman you don't love.

As scary as that is, as much as I don't want him to go, as much as I would rather run and know we'll all be safe... I also feel a swell of pride. It may not be the healthiest impulse in the world, but this man wants to protect me, and I've always wanted to be protected.

On impulse I swoop in and grab him, pulling him down for a kiss. I don't intend it to be much of one, since we need to get the hell out of here, but his big hands close around my waist, pulling me against his body, and suddenly nothing else exists. There are no cold, dank walls in a scary, abandoned warehouse. There aren't two men of questionable moral character just ahead of us, and people wanting to kill us potentially around every corner.

There's only me and Liam, his hands on my body, our tongues colliding, hearts pounding. There's nothing else. Just us.

Someone loudly clearing their throat finally pierces our moment and I pull back to see Ryder giving us a highly unimpressed look.

I can't help smiling, and Liam catches my hands, entwining our fingers as he pulls me along. Even though everything is crazy and scary and uncertain, in this moment I'm happy.

I guess I should've known.

It's not like he made it a big secret. He never came out and told me what the plan was, never explicitly answered that question when asked, but he'd given me the pieces I needed to put the puzzle together if I cared to try.

Liam was going to kill my whole family and virtually everyone I knew.

That had always been the plan. Before I arrived at the junkyard that day to steal apples, before he pinned me against the tree, before I was more than a faceless guest on a list, Liam was commissioned to engineer all of our deaths.

Once we were there, outside the house I grew up in, bustling with well-dressed partygoers and uniformed help, I had to beg him one more time not to go in. Whatever Raj had planned, just let him do it. Let the other guys do the dirty work.

It made no difference. With one last searing kiss, Liam demanded I wait in the car and he took off with Ryder and Ali, melting into the darkness. Left alone with only my nerves for company, I dug around the car and found a small pair of binoculars under the seat.

I wasn't sure I even wanted to look. As much as I wanted to accept every side of Liam, I wasn't sure I wanted to spot people I knew, knowing what Liam had planned for them.

The first several minutes of perusal turned up only strangers, but that didn't really help. They could be good people. They could have children at home in bed, waiting for them to return. Friends, parents, colleagues who would mourn them. I didn't want their deaths. I didn't want destruction on this level, not even on my worst day. I can see wanting Pietro gone, even Paul, but must there be so many casualties?

Helplessness hits me because I can't even call Liam. There's no way to reach him, to beg him to reconsider. It's too late. Theoretically I might be able to find him if I get out of the car and go creeping around, but I'm not an idiot, so I don't do that.

Suddenly, my attention is caught when I come across Paul. I'm a little floored to see he brought Marlene to *my* mother's anniversary party. He's such an ass. I feel a sliver of pity for the dumb girl, but at least she *chose* her fate. I never got that chance.

I turn my binoculars to the wooded darkness Liam and his pals disappeared into. Somewhere in the foreboding darkness, the fate I chose is preparing to risk everything—again—and I hope like hell it works out better this time than last. I'm so frustrated by his insistence on doing this, but at the same time… I sort of get it. I guess he needs to *know* the job has been finished, that Pietro doesn't survive like the cockroach he is. If we leave, he has to trust some stranger to do it, and well… Liam isn't so big on the trust thing.

I don't know how it's going to happen until I hear the first explosion. The sound's so loud that it reverberates in my chest and I duck behind the front passenger seat intuitively. Chaos ensues outside, more explosions, smaller explosions, but what really gets through, what I expect will haunt me, is the steady sound of people screaming in terror. Clapping my hands over my ears, I remain crouched on the floor. I know it's cowardly, but I can't look. I don't want a visual to accompany the sounds or the feelings.

I have to look at Liam when he comes back, after all.

The sound of gunfire explodes somewhere outside the car,

far enough away that I know I'm reasonably safe, but still so close that I can't keep from trembling. I wish they wouldn't have brought me. I know there wasn't time to take me anywhere else, but I don't want to hear what's going on out there. I don't want to be here.

It goes on forever. The screaming winds down but I remain hunched over and hiding with my eyes closed. Too many thoughts fly through my head. It feels like my heart's going to zoom right out of my chest. I'm relieved that the screaming has at least stopped, and it's sounding less like a war zone outside, until I consider what it probably means that it's getting quieter.

CHAPTER TWENTY NINE
Liam

We make it back to the car to find Annabelle in the back seat, hunched over, hiding her head in her arms like she's sick. My stomach drops. She sits up but doesn't look at me as I slide in next to her.

Ill-equipped to deal with it right now, especially in front of Ryder and Al, I ignore it for the time being. Top priority right now is getting the hell out of here.

With Ryder at the wheel and luck on our side—at least for now—we make it out. The sounds of sirens flying to the scene are behind us, and Annabelle sits beside me, worryingly silent. Not like I expected her to be a chatterbox when I got back to the car—though I suppose it could've gone that way; I can't really predict how she'll respond to things—but she still hasn't even looked at me. It's impossible to hold her to her unwitting assurance that what I did, who I was, wasn't a dealbreaker now that she's actually experienced it. I knew that. I've known it all along, every step of the way, but it still stings.

I'm not even sorry. When I fired at Paul, I knew Annabelle's tormentor was falling and felt no remorse. I didn't get Pietro, but Ryder did, and when the last breath left his body, Annabelle's world became a safer place.

I know not everyone who died tonight deserved to, but there are casualties in every war.

Now the war is over.

But now Annabelle carries the survivor's burden. I shouldn't have let her experience it. I should've made time, dropped her off somewhere and picked her up when it was all over. She would still know what I'd done, but she would've been shielded from the cold, brutal reality of being there.

Ryder finally breaks the silence. "What's the plan for tonight?"

I steal a sideways glance at Annabelle, some stupidly hopeful part of me hoping she'll look at me—but also afraid she will, and I'll see her opinion of me forever changed. Where she saw a hero before tonight, now she'll see a monster.

But she doesn't look. She remains withdrawn, arms protectively wrapped around herself, her gaze on her left kneecap.

Swallowing, I tell myself to get a fucking grip. I knew this would happen. This isn't a shock. The reaction I expected back at the mall was just late in coming; then she only heard my words, now she saw me in action. It was idiotic to let my hopes lift in the first place. I knew better.

I've always had this dormant streak of fucking absurd hope. No matter what life's dealt me, no matter what I've done, no matter how dark and realistic I've felt about the world in general, I had this sleeper cell, apparently just waiting for someone to tap into it. I'm not sure how she did it, but Annabelle has and now I'm fucked.

"Hotel," I finally respond.

"Can you be more specific? I don't know the area and we probably want something low-key where they won't ask for credit cards and license plates and all that bullshit."

I already had just such a place scoped out in case I needed it, so I tell him how to get there. About a half hour later we arrive. I send Ryder and Al in alone to reserve the rooms, leaving Annabelle alone with me. I hate that she wasn't to begin with, even if only to sit there ignoring me.

I have no idea what to expect. Deafening silence, I guess, which is how it starts. I keep an eye on the lobby door, trying to work out something to say to her.

Finally her voice, low, a little ragged, breaks the silence. "I didn't look."

I turn my head to look at her, but I don't respond 'cause I don't know how. Images pass through my mind of the kind of man she deserves, the kind of man who *would* think of things like that—cradling her head in his hands, gazing deeply into her eyes and imploring her not to look; even despite his misdeeds, seeking to protect her from having to live with visual memories of that kind of horror.

She keeps her head up, but she's looking out the windshield instead of at me. "Are they all... gone?"

Everything happened in a flurry, and I'm not positive we got every last guest, but once everyone on my list was dead, we left. Raj had brought in reinforcements and there was no time to risk letting them know they had help, but they seemed to figure out pretty quick we were firing with them, not against them. Being last minute men, maybe they thought they weren't completely filled in. At any rate, they were still picking off survivors when we left, so by the time help arrived on the scene, there's a good chance everyone was dead.

"Yeah," I tell her.

"Did you... see...?"

She doesn't finish, but I imagine she's asking about someone close to her—maybe her mother, Pietro, Paul. Before the first explosion went off, I saw her mother in the kitchen, where one of the explosives was, so I assume she was one of the first to die. I saw Ryder hit Pietro, saw the ruined, bloody suit stretched across his unmoving body. Paul's Annabelle-stand-in, Marlene, had the misfortune of being hit with a fiery piece of rubble from the explosion. Her dress caught fire and she writhed and screamed, crying out to Paul for help as he darted away. Might've been merciful to shoot her so she didn't burn to death, but I didn't.

"Everyone who hurt you is gone," I tell her.

She's quiet, but nods slightly.

It's probably not the right time, but her weird reactions seem to rub off on me and I mutter wryly, "Well, except me."

She does look over at me, but now I'm not looking at her. Maybe she was going to say something, but Ryder and Al walk out of the lobby and get back in the car, so the opportunity to speak passes. Ryder reaches over his shoulder and hands me a room key.

He parks in front of the stretch of rooms we rented out. We're all somber as we get out—even Ryder, who usually isn't, but he can read a room.

Ryder gives me an expectant look, unsure how to proceed with a chick along for the ride. I'm actually waiting on him to give me shit about it, but again, it's not the time. I need to talk to him and Al before we all part ways anyway, so I tell them I'll catch up in a minute.

Annabelle walks in front of me, then falls back so I can unlock the door to our room. I wonder if maybe I should've gotten her a room of her own, so she didn't have to be around me while she processed.

Once we're inside I tell her, "I need to go talk to them. You'll be okay here?"

She nods wordlessly and takes a seat on the edge of the drab bed.

I stand there for a minute, just watching her. I don't know what I'm waiting for. I feel tempted to ask stupid, needy questions, which is an impulse I haven't had since childhood. The vulnerability is more uncomfortable than anything else I've done tonight. I want to ask if there's anything I can do, any way I can fix this, but I don't want to hear the answer.

Without another word, without getting her to look at me, I back out of the room, securing the door and just staring at it for a moment before I turn to walk away.

I linger in Ryder's room for as long as I can. It's far from the kind of room with a mini bar, but Al disappears for a bit while I'm catching up with Ryder, and when he returns he has a six-pack of room temperature beer.

After the night we've all had, not one of us hesitates to crack that shit open.

It takes until my second can before Ryder, sprawled in his chair like he doesn't have a care in the world, finally says, "So, how the hell did this girl happen?"

The mere mention of her unsettles me. Reminds me what's waiting for me back in the other room—and not in the good way, the lusty way, though now that I'm thinking about it, my blood does stir over memories of her naked body beneath mine. I wish things could be easy. I wish the hell I've been living in since I met her could be well and truly behind us, and I could go home to her, as boring as that sounds. I just want to sink into her body and let the fucked up world around us disappear.

"Story for another time," I tell him, taking a last swig of beer and crushing the can.

"Will there *be* another time?" he asks, not unreasonably. "What's next for you?"

Shaking my head, I push off the chair and cross the room to drop the empty beer can into the small, black trash can. "Don't know. Guess I better go find out."

He stands, putting his beer down on the shoddy bedside table. "Well, I've got something in the works if you find yourself... free. You want in, I'm sure I could use one more guy."

"What kind of something?"

"The heist kind," Ryder says, grinning.

I roll my eyes. "Not my thing."

"Well, it's gonna be a big payout if you change your mind."

It makes me weary just thinking about it. I'd gotten too attached to the idea of taking a break from all this after this job was over, to a relaxed life at the beach with Annabelle, carving out something a little more normal, seeing how it fit. A heist is the last thing I want to do, but the idea of doing nothing and being alone with my thoughts after Annabelle doesn't feel right, either.

"I'll let you know," I tell him.

After I leave the guys I linger outside for a few minutes. I pretend to myself I'm being alert, keeping an eye out as I gaze at the dark, empty road, but I know I'm just avoiding Annabelle. I don't know how to comfort people, and I doubt she'd really want comfort from me right now anyhow. Even if it was the best thing I could've done for her logically, I'm sure it doesn't feel that way right now.

Eventually I run out of sidewalk to kick and phantom headlights to look for. I almost wish I smoked, I could buy myself a little more time.

Steeling myself for what's to come, I pause outside the door, take a deep breath, and finally push it open.

My eyes go to the bed, where she was when I left her, but she isn't there anymore. It's a tiny room, just a cheap bed with a nightstand, a worn beige chair. The back wall is a vanity with tacky lights overhead and a sink, because the bathroom is too small to fit one. There's a nook with a shady looking bar and some metal coat hangers off to the right of the vanity.

The bathroom door is closed and I can see the light on, so I assume she's in there. I wonder if she's physically ill. I should've been much more thoughtful, less focused on my mission and more focused on her well-being. I should've known she isn't me.

Maybe she's right. Maybe I should've stayed away and let someone else handle it. I just had to see it done, and now I'll pay the price, whatever it is. Can't say it wasn't worth it, knowing she's safe now, knowing Paul will never lay another hand on her and Pietro's reign of terror has finally ended.

Annabelle is finally free.

The bathroom door creaks as it opens up, letting a stream of light into the darkened room.

She gasps in surprise when she sees me, eyes fluttering shut, a hand flying to her chest as her whole body tenses.

I feel like I'm on trial and awaiting a verdict, but I can't bring myself to meet her eyes.

I hear her expel a breath of relief. She hesitates in front of the door for a moment, then she steps around me and heads for the bed. With her back to me, I allow myself a glimpse of her in the tiny, white towel she has wrapped around her. Droplets of water still linger across her back and shoulders, and it takes an immense measure of control not to step forward, press myself against her body, and lick them off. I imagine gripping the towel, yanking it off her, and throwing it onto the floor.

Shifting in mild discomfort, I watch her take a seat on the edge of the bed.

Her voice is a little hoarse, like maybe she's been crying. Her face is red, but I don't know what she looks like after she cries, so I don't know if it's that or the shower. Regret rocks me, knowing I'll never get to reach that level of familiarity with her.

She's looking at me expectantly and I realize I completely missed her words. "I'm sorry… what?"

Her brow furrows briefly, then with a look of concern, she asks, "Are you okay?"

"Me?" I ask, surprised. "Yeah."

She's finger-combing her hair and it's all I can concentrate on. Drops of water fall from the dark strands of her hair to the cheap carpet, and I'm hyperaware of her bare ass pressed against the bedsheet I'm going to sleep on tonight.

"Liam," she says, a little more sharply.

My eyes widen and shoot to hers and I see she's frowning again. I vaguely realize maybe she was talking again.

"I'm sorry," I tell her again, shaking my head to clear it.

Annabelle stands and pads across the short stretch until she's standing before me, her damp hair draped over her shoulder, smelling fresh and clean from the cheap bar of soap she used in the shower. Her hair doesn't carry the signature scent I've gotten used to, but she still smells amazing and I breathe her in.

"Are you okay?" she asks, her free hand coming up to skim my jawline.

I don't want to lose you. I keep the words trapped inside my tightly closed mouth, willing them to slink back down my throat and back into the abyss they crawled out of, because I'll be damned if I say that.

Doubt interrupts my defensiveness, pulling my focus to the feeling of her hand caressing my face. Comforting me.

"Are *you* okay?" I ask her, since that seems more relevant.

Her gaze drops to my chest, but her hand doesn't leave my face. It feels like she holds *my* fate in her tiny, soft hand instead of just the fate of our relationship.

Instead of answering me, she brings her eyes back to mine again and says, "In all my life, I've never known anyone who would've done what you did for me tonight."

I stare, guarded, expecting a 'but' to follow.

But... it doesn't.

Annabelle leans into me, releasing her hold on the towel. It drops on one side, then slides, and a moment later she's completely naked, the towel in a forgotten pile at her feet.

I want to touch her but I don't know if I should.

In the end, I don't have to decide, because she fists her small hand in my shirt and uses the other one to guide me until the backs of my legs hit the edge of the mattress.

Biting down on her lip, she looks tentative, but she's trying to bluff her way through it, straightening her shoulders and lifting her head before giving me a shove.

I drop to the bed, watching her. The bed creaks as she comes down on top of me, straddling my legs and pushing me back on the bed. Even though it's clear what she's doing, I can't shake the mistrust, even when she pushes her wet hair back over her shoulder and leans down to brush her lips against mine.

"What are you doing?" I ask.

She pulls back just enough to give me a sassy little smirk. "What does it look like I'm doing?"

I'm not quick enough with my answer; her hand moves between my legs and caresses my hardened arousal.

I'm not sure how to respond and I'm losing interest in words, as her hand makes a more tempting offer. I open my mouth to ask anyway, but she captures my lips with hers, and suddenly there's no more space in this cheap hotel room for words.

CHAPTER THIRTY
Annabelle

Chest heaving, I pull back to catch my breath. I'm not completely sure where I want to go with this; I only know I want him.

His hands come to rest on my hips, then slowly make their way up my sides. Excitement surges through me at the contact and I bite back a smile as he launches forward, hands creeping around to my back, until he has my breasts pressed against his face. A short moan escapes me as his mouth closes around my bare nipple.

The way he holds me close, like he's afraid he won't get to again, strikes an emotional cord. For the first time in my life, I'm completely untethered. The ties that once bound me severed by the magnificent, powerful man worshiping my body. In the space of one evening, I've experienced so much horror, so much fear and pain and devastation. I know he wrought some of it, I just don't care.

Not anymore.

I can get lost in the pain of the past, or I can move forward with a man who would put his own life at risk for me. I can focus on the terrible things he did on his way to freeing me... or I can spread my wings and soar into the future.

Our future.

Liam's hips shift beneath me and suddenly he's lifting me, switching our positions. I roll onto my back and gaze up at him, at his beautiful, strong shoulders as he hovers above me, gazing down at me like he's a lion and I'm the prey. I can't help but smile.

"Are you gonna gobble me up?" I tease.

One golden brow quirks upward and his lips curve up into a devilish little smirk. "Maybe. Is that a request?"

I open my mouth to respond but he's already moved down my body, his big, strong hands on either thigh.

"Liam, no," I say, laughing helplessly. "No, it wasn't a request. Come back up here."

Instead of obeying my request, he spreads my legs and plants himself between them. I watch his head dip, feel his warm breath on the inside of my thigh. My body tenses and I fist my hands in the sheets, anticipating contact.

Several minutes and one leg-shaking orgasm later, I'm curled up in Liam's strong arms, feeling more at peace with the world than I have a right to. I can't believe he's mine to hold. It seems unfathomable that this reserved, sometimes scary wall of blond sexiness… is mine to love.

The thought brings a smile to my face. Liam must be watching me because he shifts beneath me and says, "What?"

I tilt my head back to look up at him, toning my smile down, but unable to completely suppress it. "Hm?"

"What's the smile for?"

"You," I tell him, simply.

Despite these last few minutes, doubt still appears to be a cloud hanging over him. "I… wasn't sure how you'd feel after what you saw." Pausing a mere fraction of a second, he adds, "I'm still not… sure."

I take a moment, trying to figure out how to respond to that. It's hard to filter through all I've felt and boil it down to something simple, but I do my best. "I… I knew all along it would be something violent. Not on that scale, but… I knew. I would've probably opted out of being *right there* when it went down, but…" I pause, feeling a little self-conscious of what I'm about to admit, but then reminding myself who I'm talking to. "The thing I didn't expect was the relief."

I steal a glance up at Liam for a reaction, but as ever, the man is stoic.

I try to muster an explanation. "When it was first happening there wasn't relief. It was scary and I wanted to—to stop it, but I couldn't. It was out of my hands. And when it was over I was sort of trying to reconcile the reality of it, all those people who woke up this morning and probably had breakfast and coffee and… just lived their normal lives, with no feasible idea that they wouldn't come home from that party." I shake my head a little, not wanting to drive that home. Despite his stoicism and general aura of toughness, I'm sure some part of him must have struggled with the morality of it. I don't want to make him feel worse.

"But then… after that came the relief. Everyone who hurt me *was* gone and I didn't have to do anything. For the first time since my father died, I felt free."

He doesn't say anything right away, and even though I can't imagine he would judge me, in that moment, I fear he will. *I* sort of judged me, when the feeling first registered, and maybe he needs me to be the more virtuous partner, maybe the contrast is why we work, why he was attracted to me. Normally virtuous would be far from how I would describe myself, but compared to

Rambo over here? Yeah.

Instead of responding with words, he leans in and kisses me. My arms wind around him, craving nearness. I'm happier than I would expect to be given the circumstances, but there are still a lot of unanswered questions. Not least of which....

"Where do we go from here?" I ask, once I've pulled back enough to meet his gaze.

"You still want to go with me?"

"Well, yeah," I say with a light roll of my eyes.

He smiles, finally lowering his guard. "Yeah?"

"Without a doubt," I promise.

"Good," he replies.

I know a fishing expedition probably won't net much with him, but I try anyway with a teasing, "Oh yeah? Why is that good?"

His smile turns jaunty and he says, "Because your plane ticket wasn't refundable."

Scrunching my nose up at him, I elbow him in the side and he laughs, and I feel so damn proud of myself for making him laugh when only minutes ago it seemed like his head was a mess.

"So, the beach house?" I question.

He nods, glancing at the wall beyond me, probably piecing together our next moves. "Our flight leaves tomorrow afternoon. We'll have to stop and pick up at least a suitcase for you, just so it doesn't look weird that you're going on vacation with no belongings. I got you a fake passport, but with what just happened tonight... We don't want anyone to recognize you leaving the country tomorrow."

"That would probably be less than ideal," I agree, nodding. My thoughts get a little heavier again, wondering what could go wrong. Pietro had some cops in his pocket, but I don't know how far his reach went. What if someone *did* recognize me somehow? What if the police think I'm somehow responsible for what went down tonight?

Apparently noticing my concern, he adds, "I doubt they will. There are too many bodies to identify and with the explosions, they won't get them all, but it *was* your mother's party. In all likelihood, it will be assumed you were there."

"What's my new name?" I ask.

"Adriana White."

My eyebrows rise an inch or so. "That'll take some getting used to. Are you still Liam Hunt?"

Nodding, he says, "I had no real need to change mine. Plus my property there is in my name, and I have been there before, so people could've noticed."

I can't fight another smile, thinking of me at Liam's property. "A beach house, huh?"

His hand lazily skates up and down my arm, leaving goosebumps in its wake. "Think you can get used to that? Sand and ocean in your backyard, a covered cabana on the beach so the sun doesn't poison you in the first half hour."

"I am a little pale for the beach," I acknowledge. "We should pick up some suntan lotion."

His hand creeps around my side to my back. "And a bikini."

"I pictured you more in swim shorts, but hey, to each his own." I've barely finished my joke and he's tickling me, but it's just an excuse to touch me. I laugh and wiggle, telling him to stop, and he relents easily. I'm snug against his body by that point, and I'm so full of dreams of our future and absolute affection for this man that I feel like I must be glowing with it. Closing the distance myself, I brush my lips against his.

It's the first night of the rest of our lives, and I don't intend to waste it sleeping.

"MAFIA MASSACRE."

That's what they're calling it. I sit in the plastic seat at the airport in a dress and sandals we picked up at a thrift shop, staring up at the mounted television. An expressionless blonde newscaster offers up minimal details, throwing around words like "suspected Mafioso" and urging that while it's too soon for speculation, police are investigating.

Liam drops into the seat beside me, offering me a paper cup of warm apple cider. He's watching the television instead of me as I accept it with a murmured, "thank you," and bring the cup to my lips. It'll be hot, but he was in line for a while and we'll have to board the plane in just a few minutes.

"Should we get in line?" I ask, nodding toward the assembled lines of people lingering near

"Not yet," he says, eyes on the TV. With a nod toward it, he asks, "What's that?"

I take a casual glance around, even though it's unlikely anyone would be eavesdropping on us. There is a woman in a blue shirt who keeps staring at Liam, but by the look of things, it's because she's attracted to him. Liam picked us seats against the wall so we didn't have to sit back-to-back with strange people and chance them listening in on our conversation, anyway.

Satisfied that no one is paying attention, I'm still vague. "That mafia story we saw earlier."

"Anything new?"

I shake my head wordlessly, looking back to the television. They've moved on from the story, so I glance down at my cup and take a scalding sip.

A little lower, Liam asks, "You okay?"

Flashing him a brave smile, I say, "All good."

It does stir things up a little, seeing it on the television screen like that. Seeing footage of the house I grew up in blown to shit, hearing my life talked about as a news item.

Not my life anymore, I remind myself. That life is over, and I'm glad. I won't miss it. I won't miss any of them—I refuse.

On that note, I ask, "What happens when we get there? Are there people meeting us, or…? Will we get to see the house today?"

Nodding, he assures me, "There's a Kia Rio waiting for us at the airport."

"So we'll spend our first night in our new home tonight?" I ask, grinning.

My smile must be contagious, as he smiles, too. "We will."

The woman standing at the podium gets on her little microphone and announces that our flight will begin boarding. All the eager people already standing around begin to shuffle, but she begins to call up passengers with special circumstances first.

It's here. It's really here. None of the horrifying scenarios that played out in my head once I finally fell asleep came to pass. We made it through the airport, through security; no omniscient police force awaited us at the gates… Liam got away with it and we're making a clean getaway.

Elation moves through me, like we really are going on a vacation. This was all so impossible, too wild even to dream up, and somehow it's happening. Somehow the sexy marksman who was supposed to kill me is instead sweeping me off my feet and we're riding off into the sunset. Or, to the sunset house, at least.

Looking over at Liam, seeing a glint of a twinkle in his eye, I'm so consumed with happiness I could burst.

My life has been far from a fairy tale and I had no expectation of ever escaping it, but here it is—my happily ever after.

Liam catches me looking at him and leans in for an impulsive kiss. It's just a peck, but I grab his hand with my free one and twine our fingers together when he goes to pull back.

Sighing, gazing into my eyes, Liam tells me, "It's just gonna be you and me from now on. When we get there… it's all on us. You okay with that?"

Giving his hand a squeeze, I tell him, "I can't think of anything better."

He nods once, looking hopeful. We stand together, hands still entwined, and he grabs the suitcase with his free one. I go to grab my thrifty new purse but realize I'm still holding the apple cider. Taking one more long sip, despite the damage to my taste buds, I drop his hand just long enough to drop my cup into the nearby garbage. Once I return to Liam's side, I take his hand, and together we board the plane to paradise.

ABOUT THE AUTHOR

Sam Mariano has been writing stories since before she could actually write. In college, she studied psychology and English, because apparently she never wanted to make any money!

Sam lives in Ohio with a fantastic little girl who loves to keep her from writing. She appreciates the opportunity to share her characters with you; they were tired of living and dying in her hard drive.

Feel free to find Sam on Facebook, Goodreads, Twitter, or her blog—she loves hearing from readers! She's also available on Instagram now @sammarianobooks, and you can sign up for her totally-not-spammy newsletter!

If you have the time and inclination to leave a review, however short or long, she would greatly appreciate it! :)

Manufactured by Amazon.ca
Bolton, ON